Tommy Stands Alone

by
GLORIA VELÁSQUEZ

Piñata Books
Houston, Texas
1995

This book is made possible through a grant from the National Endowment for the Arts (a federal agency) and the Andrew W. Mellon Foundation.

Piñata Books
A Division of Arte Público Press
University of Houston
Houston, Texas 77204-2090

Piñata Books are full of surprises!

Cover illustration and design by Daniel Lechón

Velásquez, Gloria
    Tommy stands alone / by Gloria Velásquez.
      p.   cm.
    Summary: A high school student and member of a Mexican American family struggles with his sexual identity and finally learns that he will not have to stand alone anymore.
    ISBN 1-55885-146-1 (clothbound : alk. paper). — ISBN 1-55885-147-X (pbk.)
    [1. Homosexuality—Fiction. 2. Identity—Fiction. 3. Family life—Fiction. 4. Mexican Americans—Fiction.] I. Title.
PZ7.V488To   1995
[Fic]—dc20   95-13551
                                                    CIP
                                                     AC

The paper used in this publication meets the requirements of the American National Standard for Permanence of Paper for Printed Library Materials Z39.48-1984. ∞

*This book is dedicated to the memory of loved ones
AIDS has taken from us:*

*Tommy Jackson
Arturo Islas
Marlon Riggs
Lenny Jaramillo
Hilario Gallegos
Germán Larios
Frank Talamantes
Jesse Mijares
David Michael Hernández*

Tommy Stands Alone

ONE
Tommy

It's Saturday afternoon and I'm sitting on my bed sketching the new Batman from the comic book I just bought when I hear Dad's voice holler to me, "¡Tomás! ¡*Tráeme una cerveza*!" At first, I try to ignore him, thinking my mom will get him whatever he wants, but then I remember that she and my sisters went to the grocery store. Frustrated, I put my pencil down and turn my comic book over so I won't lose my page. Then I race downstairs, knowing that if I don't get Dad his beer real fast, I'll never hear the end of it.

As I walk through the dining room into the kitchen, I can see Dad sitting in the living room in his usual spot. His eyes are glued to the T.V. while he watches boxing. Opening the refrigerator door, I wonder why Dad can't do anything for himself. Does he think I'm his personal slave or what?

When I hand Dad his beer, he's careful not to take his eyes off the boxing match, not even for a second. "It's the sixth round and Gómez is winning," he tells me. I stare blankly at him. No wonder he's fat. Every weekend, all he does is drink beer and vegetate in front of the T.V. A commercial comes on and Dad finally turns to look at me. He invites me to sit down and watch the match with him. I lie, insisting that I have a book report to work on. What I really want to tell him is that I can't stand boxing, but instead I turn around and hurry back upstairs to my room and shut the door behind me.

I turn the radio on and lie back on my pillow, hoping I can forget about how much Dad gets on my nerves. But it's useless. I find myself thinking that I don't want to grow up and be like him. It seems like all he ever does is work or sit in front of the T.V., watching every single sport he can find. Don't get me wrong. It's not that I hate Dad. In a way I kinda feel sorry for him. I know that working nights at the hospital is hard. It's just that I want more out of life. I want to do something different, maybe go to college. I don't want to end up like Dad, working as a custodian all my life. Maybe I'll be a comic-book illustrator or something like that. My best friend, Maya, says I'm pretty good in Art. She's pretty sure I can get an Art scholarship when I graduate from Roosevelt High. I sure hope she's right.

When I'm finally feeling more relaxed, I reach over for my drawing. In a few minutes, I've shaded in the last part of the Batman's cape. I stare at it for a few minutes. Batman hovers over Gotham City looking ominous and powerful. It won't take me much longer to finish it. Maybe I'll show it to Maya when it's finished. Sometimes Maya and I sit next to each other in Art class. She's always snooping to see what I'm sketching. But I don't mind. Maya's pretty cool. She's the only person besides my little sisters who gets to see my sketches. Maya's good at drawing, too, except she mostly likes to draw faces of people.

María, the oldest of my two little sisters, suddenly comes bursting through the door and hollers at me, "Tomás, Dad's calling you. He wants you to help bring the groceries in." Then she disappears before I have time to yell at her for not knocking first. I slam my pencil down so hard that it pokes a hole in my drawing. Then I hurry back downstairs, wondering why it is that Dad can't get up and help. Why do I always have to do everything?

As I step into the living room, Mom comes through the front door carrying two heavy bags of groceries. I quickly take them from her and she thanks me. My youngest sister, Amanda, who is only seven-years old, is following behind with a gallon of milk. Amanda always pitches in to help, unlike María, who is two years older and makes a habit of disappearing when there's work to be done around the house.

After a few trips to the car, we finally unload all the groceries in the kitchen. Out of the corner of my eye I notice Dad still hasn't budged an inch. And he probably won't move from that spot until dinner is ready. I guess Mom must be used to him by now. I don't know. One time when I asked her why Dad never helps with things around the house, she defended him, saying he gets tired from working all week. Since then, I just keep quiet. But I don't believe her. I think he's just plain lazy.

I'm about to take off upstairs again when Dad orders me to come and watch the rest of the boxing match with him. Mom looks at me pleadingly and says, "*Ándale, hijo.* He really likes it when you watch with him." Mom knows how much I hate boxing, but even so, it's hard to say no to her. Now I know how Batman feels when he's trapped.

"Gómez is really giving it to him," Dad says as I sit down on the couch and pretend to be interested in the two moronic jerks who are busy bashing each other's heads in. Boxing is so brutal. I can't understand how anyone can consider it a sport.

An hour later, the match is finally over and María announces that dinner is ready. Dad orders me to turn the T.V. off while he heads for the kitchen. Dad always sits at the head of the table and waits for Mom to serve him. Amanda and María always argue about who gets to sit next to me.

Tonight we have fried chicken, *arroz*, *chile*, and homemade *tortillas*. Maya says my mom makes the best *tortillas* in Laguna. By the time Mom finally sits down to eat with us, her face is drawn and tired-looking. It bothers me that she has to work so hard all the time. Mom cleans houses a couple days a week for some rich ladies in town and her feet are always killing her. Someday when I'm older, I'll have a good job so she won't have to work so hard anymore.

Tonight, the dinner conversation centers on the boxing match. When Mom asks who won the match, Dad spends the next fifteen minutes describing every gory detail of how Gómez took the other guy out. I'm glad when Amanda spills her juice. While Mom cleans up the mess, I use it as an excuse to leave the table. Dad is too busy wolfing down chicken to care.

I'm almost at the top of the stairs when I hear the doorbell ring. Before I have time to go see who it is, María has beat me to it. I listen as a familiar voice greets María. It's my friend, Tyrone. All of a sudden, I'm not sure what I should do. I've been purposely avoiding him and Rudy at school. But now, there's nowhere to hide.

"Hey, Tommy," Tyrone says, coming up to the stairway.

"Hi," I answer, trying my best not to act surprised. "Come on up." I turn to María who is standing there staring at us and tell her to get lost.

"I'm gonna tell Dad on you," she warns as Tyrone follows me up to my room.

Tyrone lives in the next apartment building. We've been best friends since junior high. When I first brought Tyrone home, I remember how my parents acted 'cause he was African American. They kept staring at him, and it really made me mad. You'd think they wouldn't be prejudiced since they understand how white people are always putting us Chicanos down, but sometimes they can be just as prejudiced.

We sit down on the bed. Tyrone picks up my Batman drawing. "This is cool, Tommy," he says. "Is it the new Batman?"

"Yeah. I'm almost finished with it."

"He sure looks awesome," Tyrone says. Then he changes the subject. "Rudy and I were wondering if you wanna hang out with us at the mall tonight? Maya and Juanita are supposed to meet us there."

Maya is Tyrone's girlfriend. She's been dating Tyrone since they were sophomores. They broke up for a while when Maya was acting weird over her parent's divorce, but now they're back together.

"I'm not sure. I have a report to work on," I say, repeating the same lie I told earlier.

"Hey, what's with you, Tommy?" Tyrone asks, irritated. "Lately, you don't wanna do anything? Have you got the clap or what?"

I can feel my face turning red.

"Come on, just for a while," Tyrone begs.

I know that Tyrone won't leave me alone until I agree. Tyrone can be pushy, like my dad. "Okay," I finally mumble, and Tyrone's face breaks into a big smile.

TWO
Tommy

At seven o'clock, Tyrone and Rudy come to pick me up. I try to act excited about being with them as I climb into the back seat of Rudy's Chevy. Since Rudy lives in the same apartment building as Tyrone, they're always hanging out together. All the guys think Rudy's pretty lucky 'cause his dad lets him borrow the car whenever he wants. Rudy's a Chicano like me, except his parents were born in Mexico.

We spend the first part of the evening cruising up and down the two one-way streets downtown. Laguna is a small university city and on weekends, like tonight, the streets are crowded with college students. They like to hang out in the fancy restaurants or go bar-hopping. Laguna is filled with nightclubs, but you have to be twenty-one to go inside.

After a while, Rudy and Tyrone get tired of checking out the college girls, so we take off to the Town & Country Mall where we're supposed to meet Maya and Juanita. The mall is located on the other side of town and, since it's the only mall in Laguna, most of the teenagers like to hang out there. On the way over, I'm relieved that the radio is on so loud that I don't have to talk. I can sit back and gaze quietly out the window. To reach the mall, we have to drive around Vallejo Peak, one of seven volcanic peaks that surround Laguna. Maya says they're sacred peaks. She's into all that Indian stuff 'cause she's part Navajo. But me, I think they're pretty boring unless you're hiking up one of them.

As soon as we park the car, we head straight for the nearest entrance. Although Rudy is the oldest in our group, Tyrone is the leader whenever we're together. Sometimes it bugs me the way Rudy follows him around like a sheep dog, but then again, maybe I'm jealous. I don't know.

"Check out those babes," Tyrone says, pointing at the two girls dressed in tight-fitting shorts who are standing in front of Boo-Boo Records.

"*¡Híjole¡*" Rudy says, grinning. "I think I'm in love with the redhead."

I let out a small laugh. I know that I have to pretend to go along with them. As we walk past the two girls, Rudy whistles. Embarrassed, I notice that one of them giggles at us, but the other one flashes us a dirty look.

"I think the tall sexy one likes you," Rudy tells me.

"Oh, yeah?" I say, looking away in the opposite direction.

"Nah, she likes me," Tyrone teases back.

When we get to Pocket Change, we play some video games while we wait for Maya and Juanita. The room is filled with kids, mostly guys who are standing around like zombies pumping the machines with one quarter after another. I play a few games of Night Stalkers then walk over to watch Rudy and Tyrone play Techno-Warriors. It's the hottest video game around now. I think it's pretty violent. All that blood.

All of a sudden I feel someone tap me on the shoulder. I turn around to find Maya and Ankiza standing behind me. "Hi, Tommy," Maya says, punching me playfully in the arm. Then she moves over to Tyrone's side and says, "Get off that machine, Ty!"

"My game's almost over," Tyrone answers back.

"Where's Johnny?" Rudy asks as soon as his game ends. Rudy has been dating Juanita since last year, but her parents don't know it. Rudy and Juanita usually meet here at the mall whenever she visits Maya.

"She had to babysit. But Kizer came with me," Maya answers.

Out of the corner of my eye, I watch as Ankiza flashes everyone a big smile. Next to Juanita, Ankiza is Maya's best friend. Ankiza lives in the same fancy neighborhood as Maya. Her father is the only African American doctor in Laguna. I always thought Maya was tall, until I met Ankiza. She's a few inches taller than Maya, but she's not as skinny. Ankiza is so well-built that the guys are always whistling at her.

"Let's get something to drink." Ankiza says, interrupting my thoughts.

"Yeah, sure," Rudy agrees.

"*Ándale*," Maya says, pulling Tyrone away from his game.

At the Burger Bar, we each buy a soda and sit at one of the small round tables. I can feel people staring at us. They're not used to seeing a group of Mexicans and Blacks all at once. Especially in a city like Laguna where practically everyone is white.

As usual, Maya is the first to talk. Sometimes I wonder where she learned to be so relaxed and self-confident. "Hey, Tommy, how come you haven't been eating with us at lunchtime?" she asks me point-blank.

"It's 'cause I've been real busy," I answer right away, trying to sound as casual about it as I can. Before Maya has time to question me about what exactly has been keeping me so busy, Rudy changes the subject.

"Did you guys see *Robocop III* yet?" he asks. "Me and Tyrone saw it the other night."

Then Tyrone and Rudy start talking about the long list of bad guys Robocop kills and how some guy's eyes were shot out. They don't stop describing the violent scenes until Maya accuses them of being "Macho Maniacs." We all start laughing. Then Maya mentions that the new Bill Murray comedy will be showing at the Rialto Theater next weekend. "Why don't we all go see it together?" she asks.

Ankiza turns to look at me and says, "That would be fun. How about it, Tommy?"

Now everyone is looking at me. I feel cornered again and I'm too embarrassed to say no. "Sure," I answer, hoping that Ankiza doesn't read anything into this.

"Maybe I can bum Dad's car," Tyrone says.

"I hope Johnny can sneak out, but I doubt it," Rudy says.

"Poor Johnny," Ankiza says. "Her dad is so strict with her."

"Yeah, what a bummer," Maya says, nodding her head in agreement. Then she stands up, pulling Tyrone by the arm. "Come on. Let's go see what they have at Boo Boo's."

We all get up to follow Maya and Tyrone out to the record store. Rudy walks on ahead with Tyrone and Maya, but Ankiza slows down so she can walk next to me. I do my best to ignore her, but it's impossible. She's so pretty that all the guys going by stare at us. They probably think she's a model or something. All I know is, she's making me very nervous.

Inside Boo Boo's, I try to get away from Ankiza by going straight to the Jazz section. But my plan doesn't work because she ends up coming over to where I'm at. Still, I ignore her, moving over to the Spanish music section. She follows me again, but I pretend I'm busy examining a new CD by Banda Macho. I have no idea who they are, but I've heard them mentioned on the Spanish radio station my mom listens to. I'm relieved when Maya finally comes over and tells Ankiza it's time to go over to Montgomery Ward's to wait for her mom.

We hang out at Boo Boo's for a while longer before we finally head out to the parking lot. On the way to the car, Rudy teases me about Ankiza. "She has the hots for you."

"Shut up, *cholo*," I tell him, feeling my face turn red.

✎　✐　✐

When I get home that evening, Mom is sitting in the living room watching Don Francisco on *Sábado Gigante*. Dad is fast asleep on the couch and there are several empty beer cans on the floor next to him. I can't help but feel disgusted.

"Did you have a good time, *m'ijo*?" Mom asks.

"Yeah, it was okay," I answer, standing next to her. "What's Don Francisco up to tonight?"

"Oh, *m'ijo*, it's so sad. He was interviewing a woman whose fifteen-year old daughter ran away from home. Her mom hasn't heard from her in two years."

For a moment I feel like telling my mom, "So what? Maybe she had a good reason for doing it. Maybe her family didn't understand her. But I don't say anything. I'm always the good son."

"You better go to bed, Tomás. We have church tomorrow," Mom says softly.

"Okay, Mom," I answer, reaching down to give her a kiss on the cheek before I go upstairs.

THREE
Tommy

When Monday morning rolls around, I make sure to leave early so I can avoid walking to school with Rudy and Tyrone. It only takes about twenty minutes to get to Roosevelt from our apartments. I guess you could say we live in one of the crummiest neighborhoods in Laguna. Tyrone calls it the projects. When I was younger, I used to get embarrassed telling my teachers where I lived, but I don't anymore.

After I drop off some of my books in my locker, I go straight to the library where I sit and wait for the first-period bell to ring. Mrs. Meeker, the librarian, is always happy to see me. Everyone likes to make fun of her because she's almost six-feet tall and has the broadest shoulders. They call her the Amazon Queen. I think Mrs. Meeker's pretty nice, but I wonder what she would say if she knew that the library has become one of my favorite hiding places.

In my first two periods, I have the hardest time concentrating on what the teachers are saying. By the time I get to my third-period Math class, I find myself sketching comic book characters instead of listening to Mrs. Allen's lecture. When

the fourth-period bell finally rings, I'm relieved
that it's time to go to Art class. I don't know why,
but drawing makes me forget about all my problems.

As soon as I walk into Art, Maya signals across
the room for me to sit by her. Even though Maya is
someone I really enjoy talking to, she can be a real
pain sometimes.

"Look, Tommy, isn't she cool?" Maya says as I
come up to her side. She's pointing to a picture in
an Art book of some weird-looking woman who has
the thickest eyebrows I've ever seen and a monkey
wrapped around her shoulder. "It's Frida Kahlo,"
Maya proudly explains. "My mom says she's Mexico's most important female painter. I'm going to
sketch her."

"Oh, yeah?" I mutter, trying to act as if I'm the
slightest bit interested. Before Maya has time to
say anything else about the hairy-looking lady,
Mrs. Grant orders everyone to sit down and get
busy on their art projects. I have no choice but to
sit next to Maya.

"What a dorkhead," Maya whispers to me.

Ignoring Maya's comment, I take out my drawing pencils and a blank sheet of paper. Then I stare
aimlessly into space until Maya starts to bother me
again. "Whose portrait are you going to draw?" she
abruptly asks.

"I'm not sure," I answer, wishing that Maya
weren't so nosey. I don't know why I let her corner
me into sitting here, but then again, the class is
filled with kids I hardly know.

"Mrs. Grant said we can do a self-portrait if we
want," Maya says.

"I don't know why she gave us such a stupid
assignment," I tell her.

Maya smiles at me. "I love drawing people. I think they're the best subjects."

"Well, I hate portraits," I say, folding my arms and putting my head on the desk.

All of a sudden, Mrs. Grant is standing next to my shoulder. I instantly jerk my head up, hoping she won't lecture me about slacking off during class time.

"What have you chosen as a subject, Tommy?" Mrs. Grant asks, peering over my shoulder at the blank sheet of paper.

"I haven't decided yet," I answer, quickly picking up one of my drawing pencils.

"Better get started. This is only one project that's due before the semester ends." Then Mrs. Grant turns to talk to Maya, who has already started sketching the strange lady. "That's a great picture, Maya." Mrs. Grant leans closer so that she can examine the picture in Maya's art book. "Who's the artist?"

While Mrs. Grant is busy listening to everything that Maya knows about Frida Kahlo, I sketch a few lines on my paper. Maybe a self-portrait wouldn't be such a bad idea. I could give it to my mom for her birthday. But I don't know how I can possibly draw myself. I have such a boring face compared to other people. My cheeks are thin, my nose is pointy, and the only thing that stands out about me are my green eyes. When I was little, my mom used to call me *güero* 'cause I'm so light-com- plected. I always hated being called that.

"Hey, that's starting to look like you," Maya says, examining the outline I've drawn of my face. "Except I think your nose is pointier than that."

When I don't respond to her comments, she turns back to her own drawing and leaves me alone. But a few minutes later, Maya looks over at me and says, "I think Kizer likes you."

I feel my face start to burn, but I don't look up from my drawing, hoping Maya will get the hint.

"I think she likes your body," Maya adds, teasingly.

This time I look up at her and say, "Don't be stupid."

"I'm not kidding. Ankiza's all excited about going to the movies with you on Friday night. You're still coming with us, right?" Maya insists.

I feel a sense of relief when the bell suddenly rings and the room is filled with the noise of students getting ready to leave. I quickly stuff my drawing into my backpack and then race toward the door, hoping to get away before Maya has time to follow me. But as I head down the busy corridor, Maya runs and catches up with me.

"Wait up, Tommy," she says pleadingly, grabbing me by the arm.

I slow down, realizing that there's no way to escape Maya. What Maya wants, Maya gets.

"Tommy, please have lunch with us today," she begs. "It's no fun without you."

I shrug my shoulders and say, "Sorry, I can't." Then I take off in the direction of the next building, but Maya doesn't give up. She follows me as I head toward my locker. "Come on, Tommy. Don't be like that. Look, here comes Johnny."

As I walk up to my locker, Juanita comes over to join us. I say hello to her while Maya explains that I'm joining them for lunch today. For an instant, I feel like grabbing Maya by the shoulders and shaking her, but I don't. Instead, I have no choice but to grab my sack lunch and follow them out of the building toward the football field.

Ever since we were Freshman, we've been eating out by the bleachers. About the only time we eat inside is when it rains. But it hardly ever rains in Laguna. Sometimes we walk down to the 7-Eleven or Foster Freeze to get a soda or some junk food, but walking there takes all our lunch break, so we don't do it that often.

When we get to the football field, Rudy and Tyrone are already sitting on the bleachers eating their lunch. A few minutes later, Rina and Ankiza show up. I start to feel a little nervous because every time I look up, I catch Ankiza staring at me, but I act as if I don't notice.

Maya gets the conversation going when she starts talking about this new rap group that came out on MTV last night. Then Rina starts bad-mouthing poor old Mrs. Plumb, the Spanish teacher. We all laugh when Tyrone finally tells her to shut up. Then Ankiza looks straight at me and asks me if I can help her with her Algebra homework tonight. Before I have time to answer her, Rudy says, "Are you sure it's math you need help with?" Everyone laughs and I force myself to join in, hoping that no one notices that I'm feeling embarrassed. I'm glad when Maya and Rina start talking about music again.

After a few minutes, Rudy says, "Hey, Tyrone, did you check out David J. in P.E. today? He not only talks like a fag, he plays ball like a fag."

I feel my stomach muscles tighten, but I know I have to maintain my cool. When Tyrone laughs out loud, everyone joins him, even me. The only one who doesn't laugh is Maya.

"Shut up, Rudy," Maya says. "I like David and I don't care if he is gay."

Rudy stands up, flips his right hand down, and says, "Are you a *joto*-lover or what, Maya?"

Everyone laughs at Rudy's impersonation, only this time I don't.

"You're so damn ignorant," Maya shouts at Rudy. "My mom has a lot of gay friends. They're people just like you and me."

"Chill out, Maya," Tyrone says. "Everyone knows David's queer."

I'm starting to get angry, so I look down and pretend that I'm eating my Fritos. That's the bad thing about being a *güero*: my face turns red so easily when I'm upset. Out of the corner of my eye, I can see Maya glaring at Tyrone. But before she has time to tell him anything, the bell rings, signaling that lunch period has ended. Juanita stands up and says, "Come on, Maya. I don't want to be late for Spanish. Mrs. Plumb will have a fit.

Before any of them have time to follow after me, I take off in the opposite direction toward the gymnasium. I hear Ankiza call out goodbye to me, but I don't bother to answer her.

The rest of the afternoon, I'm too upset at myself to concentrate in my classes. Instead of listening to the teachers, I daydream about my comic-book heroes. If only I were like Batman, then maybe I would have the guts to tell Rudy and Tyrone to go to hell. Maybe then I wouldn't have to lie and pretend that I'm something I'm not.

FOUR
Tommy

All that week at school, I go out of my way to avoid meeting up with Tyrone and Rudy. It isn't easy, but I manage to keep out of their sight. During Art class, I often catch Maya staring at me as if she wants to ask me something, but instead she holds back and we end up talking about Art. As soon as the bell rings, I make sure I'm the first one out the door so that Maya doesn't have time to bug me about eating with her and the guys. It's pretty lonely eating alone and hiding out in the library, but at least I don't have to put up with their stupid remarks.

On Friday, I'm just about to head out the building for home when Ankiza stops me in the hallway and reminds me about going to the movies tonight with Tyrone and Maya. She explains that Juanita can't get out so it'll just be the four of us. Feeling nervous, I don't know exactly what to say to her. I just nod my head quietly when she tells me that we should pick them up at Maya's house at 7:30 on the dot. Then I mumble goodbye to her and disappear out the building before she has time to say anything else to me.

As I hurry through the school parking lot past the football field, I start getting more anxious and depressed. Why didn't I tell Ankiza I couldn't make it tonight? Why did I just stand there like a fool and not say anything? I guess I was secretly hoping Ankiza had forgotten all about going to the movies, but now it looks like I'm stuck. Why is it that I let everyone tell me what to do?

All the way home, I can't think of anything else, wondering how I'll ever be able to get through this evening. As soon as I walk through the front door of our apartment, Amanda comes running up to me. "Hi, *gordita*," I tell her with a faint smile. Mom says that Amanda looks a lot like me when I was her age. She has the same green eyes and caramel-colored hair that I do, while María, with her dark brown hair and skin, looks more like my mom.

"Want to color with me?" Amanda asks, showing me her new coloring book. Amanda loves it when I sit down and color with her, but it makes María real jealous.

"Later, *gordita*," I answer, heading straight for the kitchen where Mom is busy making fresh *tortillas* for Dad to take in his lunch pail. Dad works the four-to-midnight shift at Laguna Hospital.

"Hi, *m'ijo*. How was school today?" Mom asks, looking up from the stove. María is sitting at the table eating a taco.

"It was okay," I answer, grabbing a *tortilla* from the pile on the table.

"There's beans, too, *m'ijo*," Mom says.

"Nah, that's okay," I say, grabbing a Coke from the refrigerator.

"How come he can have a Coke and not me?" María asks in a whiny voice.

I flash her a dirty look as I take a quick bite of my *tortilla*. Suddenly the doorbell rings, and before I have time to take off upstairs, Amanda comes into the kitchen followed by Tyrone. I feel a sinking sensation in the pit of my stomach.

"Hello, Mrs. Montoya," Tyrone politely greets my mom. Then he looks at me and says, "Tommy, I just wanted to let you know that Dad lent me his car so we can pick up our dates tonight."

Before I have time to react to Tyrone's statement, Dad comes walking into the kitchen. He's wearing his drab, gray janitor's shirt that I absolutely detest. "So you boys have dates tonight?" he asks Tyrone.

"Yeah, Mr. Montoya. We've got two chicks lined up for tonight."

Dad's face breaks into a big smile and he turns to me, saying, "*Ay*, Tomás. I guess we better have a talk about women. Who's the lucky *ruca*?"

I can feel myself start to blush. For a moment, I want to reach over and smack Dad until the grin disappears from his face. But I know that I can't. "Just a friend from school," I whisper.

Then María starts to repeat, "Tommy has a girlfriend. Tommy has a girlfriend," and she doesn't stop until Mom orders her to keep quiet.

"*Bueno, vieja*. Time to go," Dad says, grabbing his lunch pail from the table. But before he leaves, Dad pulls out his wallet and hands me a $20 bill. "Here. So you can keep the little girls happy."

It takes all of my self-control to keep from telling Dad off as he leaves the kitchen. Sometimes Dad can be such a pig. I don't understand how Mom can put up with him.

"Your dad's pretty cool," Tyrone tells me. "Listen, I have to go. I'll pick you up at seven."

"Sure," I mumble, walking Tyrone to the front door. Then I hurry upstairs to my room, feeling more hopeless than ever.

✎   ✏   ✐

When Tyrone comes to pick me up at seven, I pretend that I'm excited about going out with Ankiza. On the drive over to Maya's house, all Tyrone talks about is girls. Next to music and the Lakers, that's the only thing he ever thinks about. He spends most of the ride over telling me about this girl at school who sleeps around with all the guys. Then he laughs and tells me that she finally got knocked up by some guy he knows. I can't help but think to myself that Tyrone can be a real creep, like a lot of other guys.

When we arrive at Maya's house, we both get out of the car and walk up to the front door. Maya lives in a beautiful split-level house on the wealthy side of Laguna. She says it bugs her that there aren't any Chicanos or African Americans in this neighborhood, except for Ankiza's family.

As soon as we ring the doorbell, Maya's mother opens the door. "Hi, Tommy. Hi, Tyrone. Come on in," she says with a warm smile. Maya's mom is real nice and pretty. She likes for us to call her by her first name, Sonia, because she says she feels real old when we call her Mrs. Gonzales. I haven't seen her since last year when I used to come over a lot to help Maya with her Algebra.

I can't imagine living in a house like Maya's. It's so huge, compared to the tiny apartment we live in, but I guess that's because Maya's parents have a lot of money. Maya's mom is a professor and her dad's an engineer. I sure wish my dad could have gone to college. Even though he was born here in California, he never even graduated from high school. Dad said he had to drop out in the 8th grade to help his mom and dad, who worked in the fields. My mom didn't graduate either. But I'm going to make sure I graduate and go to college.

"The girls are almost ready," Sonia says as we step inside the hallway.

Before we have time to start talking, Maya and Ankiza appear before us.

"Hi, guys," Maya says cheerfully.

Ankiza looks over at me and I say hello to her. I'm feeling very awkward, wishing I didn't have to go through with this. But I know there's no way out.

"Now, Maya, don't forget," Sonia reminds her, "you need to be home by 11:30 sharp."

"I know, Mom. You already reminded me a thousand times," Maya answers back as we rush out the door. Then she turns to me, saying, "I sure wish I were a guy so that I could stay out as late as I want."

"I'm sure glad you're not, babe," Tyrone says, putting his arm around Maya and pulling her close to him.

When we get to the car, I open the door for Ankiza and then I climb into the back seat after her, sitting as close as I can to the door. I can't help but notice how close Maya sits to Tyrone. It's a wonder he can even drive with one arm on the wheel and the other around Maya.

Maya and Tyrone do most of the talking. Ankiza doesn't say much except when Maya asks her a question. After a few moments, Ankiza turns to me and says, "How come you haven't been around at lunchtime, Tommy?"

I can feel the lie starting to form inside my head. "I've been real busy," I answer her. "I have this long report to do." I wonder if Ankiza can tell that I'm making up a story.

"We really miss you," Ankiza says gently.

"Speak for yourself," Maya yells back while Tyrone starts to laugh. I manage to force out a smile.

Downtown, we get lucky and find a parking space that is only a few blocks away from the theater. When we get to the ticket booth, there is no one standing in line. Tyrone insists on paying for Maya's ticket, even though she protests. So I do the same and pay for Ankiza.

At the snack bar, we stock up on popcorn, sodas and candy and then go inside the theater to look for a place to sit. It's dark because the previews have already started and it takes us a few minutes to find a row with four vacant seats. The movie turns out to be pretty funny, and it almost makes me forget how nervous and uncomfortable I'm feeling. Bill Murray is hilarious. He plays a cop who's a vampire. He spends most of the movie going around biting criminals.

Halfway through the movie, Ankiza reaches over and puts her hand over mine. I'm not sure how I should react, so I don't do anything. I just stare straight ahead at the film, pretending it doesn't bother me. Out of the corner of my eye, I can see Tyrone making out with Maya. I wonder how I ever let myself get talked into this.

When the movie finally ends, Maya and Ankiza insist that it's their turn to treat us, so we walk across the street to Pizza Hut. It's crowded when we get there, but after a few minutes we manage to get a table in the back. I'm not as nervous about sitting next to Ankiza, since it's a big round table.

While we eat, we talk about the funniest part of the movie where Bill Murray finds out his cop girlfriend is also a vampire. Then Maya tells us about the car her dad is buying her this year, insisting that we can all pile into it and drive to the beaches in Santa Barbara. Tyrone teases Maya and tells her that she's spoiled, but Maya playfully punches him in the arm.

After we finish eating, Tyrone asks if any of us would like to drive out to the beach, but I make up a story about how I need to go home and babysit my two little sisters. Ankiza looks at me in a funny way, as if she knows I'm lying, but she doesn't ask me any questions. Instead, she tells Maya that she also needs to go home early.

We drive over to Ankiza's house first. When we get there, I politely get out of the car and walk Ankiza to her front steps. Before she opens the door to go inside, she smiles at me and says, "Thanks, Tommy. I had fun, even though I know you were kinda forced into this."

I stand there awkwardly. I don't want to hurt Ankiza's feelings. After all, she's always been a good friend, like Maya. "I had fun, too," I finally tell her, and Ankiza leans over and gives me a light kiss on the cheek.

Back in my room that night, I have a hard time falling asleep because I can't stop thinking about my date with Ankiza. I wonder what she would say if she knew. I wonder if she would still want me for her friend. If I only had more guts, then maybe I wouldn't have to lie and pretend all the time.

FIVE
Tommy

By Monday, I'm anxious to get back to school. Weekends are a real drag when Dad's around. We all have to put up with watching everything that he likes on T.V., from old reruns of *Gilligan's Island* to wrestling, which I absolutely detest. It's so phony. And what makes me even sicker is how Mom waits on Dad hand-and-foot. *"¿Quieres algo, viejo? Sí, viejo. No, viejo."* It makes me want to puke, listening to her cater to his every need.

When the fourth-period bell rings, I start to dread going to Art class. I know that Maya is going to start bugging me about Friday night. I take my time getting to class, but as soon as I step inside, Maya corners me and starts to give me the third degree.

"Ankiza said she really had fun on Friday."

"Yeah, it was all right," I answer, trying to sound uninterested while I take out my art supplies.

"All right...that's all?" Maya repeats incredulously. "Ankiza will have a heart attack when I tell her you said she was all right."

This time I smile a little. Maya can be so dramatic. "Yeah, all right," I repeat.

Before Maya has time to bug me some more, Mrs. Grant raps her ruler on the desk, ordering everyone in the class to get busy. Maya whispers something to me, but I pretend I don't hear her as I start to work on my self-portrait. It's beginning to look more and more like me. Except for the nose. I'm not quite sure whether it's too small or too large. I'm about to make it smaller when Maya leans over my shoulder and says, "That's good Tommy. It looks just like you."

"You don't think the nose is too big?"

"Nope. You're a *narizón*, just like me. That's all there is to it."

"At least I don't have one long eyebrow, like your Frida," I tease her back.

Maya and I start to laugh, and we don't stop until Mrs. Grant gives us one of her mean get-to-work looks. Maya whispers something under her breath as we turn our attention back to our drawings.

I'm so immersed in my self-portrait that I forget to keep an eye on the time. When the lunch bell suddenly rings, I hurry and gather up my art supplies, hoping to race out of the classroom before Maya has time to follow me. Just as I am about to go out the door, Maya reaches over and grabs me by the arm.

"Tommy, don't move. You're eating with us today."

I'm about to protest when Ankiza, Juanita and Rina come walking up to us. They all smile when Maya tells them I'm joining them for lunch. Frustrated because I've been cornered once again, I start to walk with them.

After we stop by our lockers, we walk out to the bleachers to meet Rudy and Tyrone. Maya and

Juanita sit on the same row as Rudy and Tyrone, while Ankiza, Rina and I sit right below them.

As always, the girls get the conversation going. Rina tells everyone the most recent horror story about her stepdad and how she can't stand him. Then she and Maya start to make fun of Mrs. Plumb, the Spanish teacher. Maya tells everyone how she was playing around with Charley in Spanish and she called him *"El Rey de Los Pedos"* or the King of Farts. When Mrs. Plumb heard Maya say that, she asked what *pedos* meant and Charley explained to her that it was the name of a small town in Baja California. Then Charley told Mrs. Plumb that she could be the queen or *"La Reina de Los Pedos."* We all start laughing, and I feel the tension around my shoulders start to loosen up. It dawns on me that it feels pretty good being with my friends. On an impulse, I reach over and grab Maya's Ding-Dong out of her hand before she has time to unwrap it. Then I toss it over to Rudy and he tosses it up in the air. By the time it gets back to Maya, it's all smashed. *"¡Cochino!"* Maya yells at me, and I'm suddenly feeling like my old self.

When the fifth-period bell rings, we all start to moan as we gather up our stuff. I'm bending down to pick up my back pack when I feel something fall out of my shirt pocket. Before I have time to pick the folded note up from the ground, Rudy grabs it. *"Ay,ay,ay,* What's this?" he says, unfolding the note.

"Give it back," I yell, trying to grab it out of his hand, but Rudy jumps back up on the bleachers and starts to read out loud. *"Dear Tommy, I'm really sorry your dad acts like that. Sometimes my dad gets on my case, too. Don't forget, any time you need somebody to talk to, just give me a call. David J."*

By now, my face is burning hot and everyone's
eyes are on me. My mouth starts to feel very dry
and I want to get away from here as quickly as possible, but my body is frozen, unable to move.

"Is this from David, the *joto*?" Rudy asks, crum-
pling the note up and throwing it at my face.

Then Tyrone asks me point-blank, "Are you a
faggot or what, Tommy?"

In a loud voice, Maya tells Tyrone to shut up
while Rina and Juanita start to laugh. Ankiza low-
ers her head and doesn't say a word.

It seems as if minutes go by instead of seconds,
but from somewhere deep inside of me I manage to
gather the strength to pick up my backpack and
take off walking across the football field. In the
background, I can hear Maya calling after me, but I
don't slow down until I'm several blocks away from
Roosevelt. Angry and confused, I continue to walk,
not knowing exactly where I'm going. The only
thing I know is that I want to get as far away as
possible from school. I hate my friends. I hate
myself. I hate everything about my life.

It isn't long before I find myself circling hopelessly around the side streets of the downtown area.
I'm glad there aren't too many people shopping at
this time of day. As I walk past a clothing store, my
reflection stares back at me from the window. My
eyes fill with tears. I want to throw something. I
want to break the glass into a thousand pieces so I
won't ever have to see myself again.

I keep on walking until I suddenly find myself
at Laguna Park. I find a secluded spot away from
the playground and sit down, hoping to calm myself
down. My head is throbbing badly and I feel uglier
than I've ever felt in my life. Why didn't I speak up
and say something to Rudy? Why did I just stand

there and let them laugh at me and call me names? How could I have let them say those things about me and David? After all, David is just a friend. But now, they're all going to spread rumors and lies about us. If only I had somewhere to hide. If only I had enough money, I could go to my grandma's in Texas.

I don't know how much time passes while I sit there, solitary and alone, wanting to disappear off the face of the earth. When a school bus goes by, I know that school has ended, and I start to feel panicky. I'm not sure what I should do next, where I should go. This is the first time I've ever cut classes. Then all of a sudden, I remember Snowball, the wino who lives on the other side of my apartment building. I get up quickly, knowing exactly where I'm headed.

By the time I get back to our apartment complex, it's almost 4:00 and I know that Dad has already left for work. I take the long way around through the back, making sure no one sees me as I approach Snowball's apartment.

As soon as I knock, Snowball opens the door. His face is puffy and red and he smells bad. "*Quihúbole, Tomás,*" Snowball greets me in a slurred voice.

"Hi, Snowball. Can I come in?" I hear myself ask him.

Snowball nods his head, and I follow him into the small living room. There are empty beer bottles lying everywhere and the room smells like liquor. Although this is the first time I've ever been inside Snowball's apartment, it seems familiar because the floor plan is just like our apartment. I don't know much about Snowball except that he lives alone and people say he's been a drunk ever since his son was killed in Vietnam. Dad's always warning me to stay away from him, saying he's a no-good wino who buys booze for all the underaged kids.

"Snowball," I begin hesitatingly, "I was wondering if I could buy some booze off of you?"

Snowball gives me a long hard look as he reaches out for the quart of beer on the coffee table. Then he signals for me to sit down on the dirty couch as he disappears into the kitchen. A minute later, he reappears with a bottle of vodka. "*¿Estás seguro*? Tomás?" he asks, handing me the bottle.

I nod my head yes, quickly taking the bottle from his hand and stuffing it inside my backpack. Then I give him the $5 he asks for and head back out the door before he has time to say anything else to me.

Once I've checked to make sure that Dad's car is gone, I hurry through the front door of our apartment, hoping that Mom won't give me the third-degree for being late. I mumble "hello" to María and Amanda, who are sitting on the couch watching cartoons. As I start to climb the stairs, Mom pokes her head out of the kitchen and asks me why I'm late. Very calm-like, I tell her that I had to go to the library. Then she tells me that she made some fresh *tortillas*, but I tell her I'm not hungry, insisting that I need to get started on my homework.

Upstairs, I sneak into the bathroom. I carefully open the medicine cabinet and take out several bottles of pills. After I stuff them in my pockets, I go straight back to my bedroom, locking the door behind me. I turn the radio on and slowly take the bottle of vodka out of my backpack, knowing what I must do. I know there's nowhere to run. Nowhere to hide.

SIX
Ms. Martínez

I was just about to sit down at the table and enjoy some of Frank's delicious spaghetti when the phone started ringing. I hesitated, anticipating Frank's reaction. He hated it when someone called at dinnertime, especially when he was the one who had prepared the night's meal.

"Go ahead, but make it short," Frank warned.

"See why we need an answering machine?" I said, reaching for the phone on the kitchen wall. For the past month, I had been hopelessly trying to convince Frank that we needed to invest in an answering machine, but for some odd reason he wouldn't hear of it.

"Hello," I answered, hoping it wasn't one of my distraught patients.

"Hi, Ms. Martínez. It's me, Maya."

"Oh, hello, Maya. How are you?" I asked, trying not to sound too surprised. I hadn't talked with Maya since she and Sonia had returned from their Christmas trip to New Mexico. According to Sonia, who was a good friend of mine, things were going very well for Maya at school.

"I'm doing real good."

"I'm so glad to hear that." I waited for Maya to continue, but there was dead silence on the line. Then I heard some muffled sobs in the background. "Maya, what's wrong?" I asked gently, signaling for Frank to scoot a chair over to me so that I could sit down.

It took Maya a few minutes before she was finally able to answer. "It's not me, Ms. Martínez," she whispered. "It's my friend Tommy."

I immediately ran the names of Maya's and Juanita's friends through my mind, hoping to recall which one was Tommy, but for the life of me I couldn't picture him. "Tommy?" I repeated into the receiver, hoping that I wasn't sounding too obvious.

"Yeah, Ms. Martínez. Tommy's in a lot of trouble," Maya said, releasing a few more sobs before she continued. "He's in the hospital. He tried to kill himself yesterday."

"Oh, my God," I said, running my hand through my hair. "Is he all right?" I asked, feeling the tension start to mount around my shoulders.

"Yeah, he's going to be fine. But it was real awful."

"How did it happen?" I forced myself to ask Maya.

"I guess he locked himself up in his room and took a bunch of pills and alcohol. He's been real depressed lately. He called me right after he took all the pills, so I called his mom right back and told her what was going on. She called 911 right away. They say Tommy was lucky because they got him to the hospital in time."

I held my breath for a moment, not wanting to speak, not wanting to think about my teenage brother Andy. If only he'd had a friend like Maya.

Maybe then someone would have saved him from taking his life.

"What can I do to help?" I asked, chasing the thought of Andy's death away.

"Well, Ms. Martínez, I was wondering if you would go to the hospital with me and talk to Tommy. He really needs someone to talk to."

"Yes, of course, Maya. What hospital is he at?"

"He's at General Hospital. Do you think we could go tonight?"

I glanced over at Frank who was already devouring a second serving of spaghetti. Frank would understand, I thought to myself. He knew how much I cared about Maya.

"Sure," I answered. "Why don't I pick you up in an hour?"

"Thanks, Ms. Martínez," Maya whispered. Some of the tension had left her voice.

After I hung up the receiver, I pulled my chair back to the table to join Frank, who was busy wiping up the left-over sauce from his plate with a slice of garlic bread.

"Sorry," I said, helping myself to some spaghetti.

Seeing the strained look on my face, Frank asked, "What is it hon? Is Maya all right?"

I gazed into Frank's sea-blue eyes, admiring his finely chiseled nose and the head filled with golden curls. Frank hated his natural curly hair and he was always telling me how much he wished he had straight Indian hair.

"Maya's fine," I finally answered in a tired voice. "But one of her friends from school—Tommy—tried to take his life. Maya was calling to see if I would go with her to the hospital and try to talk to him."

"I'm sorry, hon," Frank said, reaching over and patting my hand. "I know how this must remind you of Andy."

My eyes started to fill with tears. "Yes, it does," I replied, pausing for a moment to regain my composure. "But, I'll be fine. It's Tommy I'm concerned about. I told Maya I'd pick her up in an hour and we'd go over to the hospital to see him. I hope you don't mind."

"It's okay, hon. I know you want to help. Would you like me to drive you both over there?"

I'd never met anyone as thoughtful and unselfish as Frank. He was always willing to help out, especially when it concerned my family or my friends. I guess that's why I loved him so much.

"Thank you, Frank. That's so sweet of you, but I'll be fine. Besides, you've eaten so much, you probably won't be able to move."

Grinning, Frank patted the small bulge around his stomach. "But don't you think I'm a sexy *panzón?*"

I had to laugh out loud at Frank's Spanish. Over the years, he had picked up a few key words and phrases from being married to me, and he always managed to use them in a funny way. "*Ay,* Frank, *estás bien loco,*" I said, taking another mouthful of spaghetti.

✎   ✐   ✎

As soon as I pulled up to the driveway, Maya came running out the front door. Although her eyes were puffy and red, Maya greeted me cheerfully as she climbed into the front seat. "Hi, Ms. Martínez. Before I forget, my mom said to tell you hi. She had to go to back to campus tonight."

"Say hello for me," I said, backing out of the driveway and heading down the street. "Are you feeling a little better?"

"I guess so. It's just that Tommy is one of my very best friends, and I think I know why he took all those pills."

"And why is that?" I asked, turning onto the freeway.

"Well, on Monday at lunchtime, Rudy found a note this guy named David wrote Tommy. David's gay, so Rudy and Tyrone started calling Tommy a queer, and everyone started to laugh at him."

"I see," I whispered, waiting patiently for Maya to continue her story. After giving it some thought, Maya finally blurted out, "You see, Tommy's gay, too, but he doesn't want anyone to know about it."

Suddenly, it was all starting to make sense. "Did Tommy tell you he's gay?" I asked softly.

"Yeah, Ms. Martínez. He did...on the phone the night he tried to kill himself. I...we all didn't know. But I don't care. I like Tommy for who he is. I don't care if he's gay. That's what I told him on the phone that night. But I don't know what he...we can do. Almost everyone I know at school hates gays, especially now with AIDS going around."

"Yes, I understand, Maya."

"I'm just hoping Tommy will talk to you, Ms. Martínez. He desperately needs someone to talk to, and you've always been so cool about everything," Maya said, turning to look at me again.

"Thanks for your vote of confidence, Maya. I'll do the best I can. But, you know Tommy has to want to talk to me. I can't force it out of him. And I'm a stranger."

"Yeah, I know," Maya sighed. She sounded so hopeless and sad that I reached over and patted her on the hand.

✎ ➱ ✎

At the hospital, the receptionist gave us Tommy's room number and pointed us in the direction of the elevator. We got off on the third floor and followed the arrows down the corridor until we came to a small visitor's lounge.

"Why don't I wait here while you visit with Tommy first," I told Maya. "I think you should let him know that I'm here."

"Okay, Ms. Martínez," Maya agreed. Then she disappeared down the corridor in search of Tommy's room.

The visitor's lounge was empty except for an older gray-haired woman who was sitting in an armchair crocheting some sort of afghan. She looked up and smiled at me as I sat down on the vinyl couch across from her. I politely said hello to her. Then I reached over for a copy of *People* magazine from the end table to busy myself with while I waited for Maya's return. I was almost finished with an article on Tom Cruise when Maya appeared at the doorway.

"You can come with me now, Ms. Martínez," she said.

I quickly put the magazine down and walked over to her side. "How did Tommy react when you told him I was here?"

"He didn't say much. But I know he was surprised. He doesn't look so good."

"That's to be expected," I said, following Maya down the busy hallway and into Tommy's room.

It was a typical hospital room with two beds separated by a white plastic curtain. A man in his early thirties appeared to be asleep in the first bed. Tommy's bed was on the far end of the room, next to the window.

"Tommy, this is Ms. Martínez," Maya said as we came up next to his bed.

When Tommy turned his head to look at me, I was taken aback by his resemblance to my brother Andy. He was fair-skinned with the same light-colored hair as Andy had that fell in a wave across his forehead.

"Hello, Tommy," I said gently, noticing how pale and fragile he looked. "I'm glad we finally get to meet. Maya's told me what good friends you two are."

"Oh, yeah," Tommy mumbled, looking away from me.

The room filled with silence while we both waited for Tommy to say something else. Finally, Maya broke the silence. "I need to go *pipí*. I'll be right back, Tommy." I right away moved closer to Tommy's side, hoping this was the right moment to talk to him alone.

"Tommy," I began speaking very cautiously. "Maya told me what happened, and I'm very concerned. I'd like to try to help, if you'll let me. I have an office downtown and I'd be willing to meet with you whenever you'd like so we can talk about what happened. I know you don't know me, but I believe I can help you."

Tommy was staring intensely at me and I could see the hurt in his eyes.

I reached over and patted his hand. "I know things don't look very bright right now, Tommy, but I know with some help, things will get better."

Before I could say anything further, Tommy said, "Thanks, but I don't need any help." Then he turned to look away from me.

"Please think about it, Tommy," I continued, ignoring his rejection. "Just in case you do change your mind, here's my card. It has both of my phone numbers on it. And you can call me at home anytime you want."

Tommy mumbled thanks as I placed the card on the table next to him. Just then Maya came walking back into the room. "Hey, Tommy. How 'bout a Big Mac? I can sneak one in the room if you want!" she teased.

A faint smile appeared on Tommy's face. I knew it was a good time for me to make a quick exit. But before I left, I reminded Tommy to call me if he changed his mind. Then I went back out to the waiting room to wait for Maya.

SEVEN
Ms. Martínez

Driving home that evening, I kept thinking about how much Tommy reminded me of my brother Andy, and suddenly I was consumed by all the awful memories of his death. It was a night that was permanently etched in my mind. I was a student at Fresno State University, and my best friend Priscilla and I had gone to see a movie that evening. I remember that it was a romantic love story and that we both cried at the end. After the movie we had gone to a nearby cafe where we ran into some other friends and sat around talking about meaningless things. By the time I got back to my apartment, there was a message from my roommate that my *Tía* Luisa had called several times. My first reaction was fear because *Tía* Luisa only called when there was an emergency back home. When I was finally able to get through the busy telephone line, *Tía* Luisa instructed me to come home right away because there had been a terrible accident and Andy was dead.

Badly shaken, I drove back to Delano that same night. When I arrived, the house was filled with relatives and neighbors. Dad was sitting on the couch, looking distant and sad, unable to speak

or even notice I was there. Mom was in bed heavily
sedated from the pills the doctor had given her to
calm her down. Only *Tía* Luisa seemed to notice or
even care that I was suffering just as much as my
parents.

In the days that followed, I clung to *Tía* Luisa's
side, mourning the loss of my only brother. It
wasn't until much later that the police notified us
that they suspected Andy's death had been a suicide. According to medical reports, there had been
a mixture of cocaine and alcohol in Andy's blood at
the time of the accident. The police further
explained that the car's skid marks revealed that
Andy had purposely driven the car at a high speed
directly into the utility pole.

My parents never said a word to me about
what the police report had uncovered about Andy's
death. They buried their grief deep inside, shutting
me out completely. This made me even crazier. No
way would I accept what the police had told us.
Andy was only sixteen, a model student. He
wouldn't take his own life. I was sure of that. It
must be a mistake, I kept telling myself. Later,
when the shock had finally worn off, I felt I had no
other choice but to face the truth. I even spoke with
Andy's best friend, Tony, who told me that Andy
had mentioned that afternoon at school that he felt
like killing himself. But Tony had thought Andy
was joking around. Slowly I began to piece everything together, thinking back to my last visit home.
Andy had barely spoken to me. He had stayed
locked in his room most of the weekend, but I had-
n't made anything of it, thinking his behavior was
due to teenage hormones. Yet the truth had been
right there, staring me right in the face—all those
endless years of Dad's drunken binges, midnight

runs to half-way houses, and Mom's aching heart. Only I was the lucky one. I had been able to escape it all. Not Andy. He had been too young to run away like me.

   ✎ ✏ ✐

When I walked through the front door, Frank was lying on the couch watching the Comedy Channel. How I envied the fact that he could spend hour after hour listening to one comedian after another. If only I had grown up in a family like Frank's that loved to laugh and tell silly jokes.

"Hi, honey," Frank said, sitting up and lowering the sound on the T.V. "How did it go? How's Tommy?"

I kicked off my shoes and sat down next to him. "Well, it didn't go all that well. Tommy hardly said a word to me, and he looks very depressed. I couldn't get him to talk."

"What about Maya? Did he open up to her?"

"Somewhat, but I guess he was very distant with her, too."

"I'm sorry," Frank said, tightening his arm around my shoulder. "Does Maya have any idea why he tried to kill himself?"

"You're not going to believe it. According to Maya, the kids at school found a note that some boy who's gay wrote to Tommy. And they all started making assumptions about Tommy being gay."

"Is Tommy gay?"

"I guess he is. Anyway, that's what he told Maya the night he took all the pills."

"Oh, my God," Frank said. "Now I understand why he would try to take his own life. So many people have no qualms about expressing their hate or fear of homosexuals."

"I know. There's so much homophobia around. And teenagers can be especially cruel when they suspect someone is gay. Tommy's probably been trying to keep it a secret for who knows how long."

"I remember when my brother Bryan told us he was gay. We were all shocked, especially Dad. We couldn't believe that he had kept it a secret for almost twenty years. Now, of course, we make jokes about it. But I know it was tough for Bryan to keep it a secret through high school and college."

"Having someone who's gay is one of the most difficult things for a family to accept. And if being macho is a family value, it's even worse."

"Aren't you glad I'm not a macho man?" Frank suddenly teased, lifting up his right arm so he could flex his muscles up and down.

"Ay, Frank," I exclaimed, pushing his arm out of the way. "I only hope it's not too late for Tommy like it was for Andy."

Frank reached over and wiped away the tear that was sliding down my cheek. "Don't worry, hon," he said. "Tommy will be fine, just you wait."

EIGHT
Ms. Martínez

The next day, after I had finished my last appointment, I drove over to search for Tommy's apartment. According to Maya, Tommy lived in the same apartment complex as Juanita, only a few minutes from my office. As soon as I turned onto Cabrillo Street, I recognized the dirty brown two-story buildings where most of Laguna's poor families lived, the majority being Chicanos, Puerto Ricans and African Americans. Why was it that every city in the United States had to have its *barrio* or ghetto where people of color were marginalized from the rest of the society? It just didn't seem fair.

After I located the building where Tommy lived, I parked my car across the street, noticing that Juanita's apartment was only a couple of buildings over. As I opened the car door, I wondered if Juanita had been one of the friends who had humiliated Tommy. I wanted to believe that she, like Maya, had stood by him. After all, Tommy was going to need all the friends he could find.

As soon as I knocked on the front door, a pretty little girl with light-colored hair like Tommy's opened the door.

"Who are you?" she asked, wrinkling her small button nose at me.

"Well, hello," I replied, smiling. "My name is Sandra, Sandra Martínez. Is your mom or dad home?"

Before the tiny girl had time to answer me, a slightly taller dark-skinned girl appeared in the doorway. "Go call Mom, stupid," she said, pushing her little sister out of the way.

"Stop it, María," the younger sister called back as she disappeared from sight.

"You must be Tommy's sister?" I asked the dark-eyed María. She stared intensely at me.

"You know my brother?" she asked, puzzled.

"Yes. I'm a friend of his."

All of a sudden, María stepped aside to make room for her mother. "María, have you forgotten your manners? Come in, please," said the short, pretty woman with friendly eyes, who reminded me a great deal of my own mother.

Inside, I held out my hand to Mrs. Montoya and introduced myself for the third time. She politely shook my hand and invited me to sit down. As I sat down on the couch, I recognized the layout of the apartment. It was the same as Juanita's. The first floor consisted of a medium-sized living room which connected to a very small dining room that led into the kitchen. The bedrooms and bathroom were all upstairs.

Before she sat down, Mrs. Montoya turned to the two little girls who were standing next to her, watching me suspiciously, and ordered them in Spanish to go upstairs. Reluctantly, they both turned around and disappeared up the stairway.

Mrs. Montoya was staring nervously at me, so I decided I better let her know why I had come. "Mrs.

Montoya," I began, "you're probably wondering why I've come to see you. I'm a friend of Maya Gonzales and her family. Yesterday, Maya called and asked me to accompany her to the hospital to visit your son Tommy, which I did. The reason Maya wanted me to visit him is because I'm a psychologist. I've helped Maya and her friends when they've had problems."

A worried, tired look appeared on Mrs. Montoya's face, but she remained silent. I decided to continue. "I wanted to meet you and your husband so I could let you know that I'm willing to help Tommy. I know how you both must be feeling after finding out that your son tried to take his own life."

Mrs. Montoya sat up straight and in a tense, anguished voice replied, "It was all an accident. Tomás told me it was an accident, that he didn't mean to do it."

"Do you really believe that, Mrs. Montoya?" I asked gently, hoping not to scare her.

I noticed the tiny wrinkles form around the corners of Mrs. Montoya's eyes as she quickly came to her only son's defense. "Tomás would never try to do anything to hurt himself. He's a good boy."

"Does Mr. Montoya feel the same way as you, that it was an accident?"

There was a brief moment of silence before Mrs. Montoya finally answered my question. "He doesn't know. He thinks Tommy has pneumonia. He works nights so he wasn't here when it happened."

Lies. Little white lies. Anything to avoid pain. My heart went out to Mrs. Montoya. It was all so typical, so unavoidable. The strong Mexican woman trying to protect her family. "Don't you think it would be better for everyone if Mr. Montoya knew the truth?" I asked.

Mrs. Montoya slouched back in the chair, letting out a deep sigh. "No. It's better this way. Anyway, it was just an accident. Tomás will be fine."

I could tell by the distraught look on Mrs. Montoya's face that she wasn't totally convinced by her own words. Yet I knew it would be futile to sit here and try to change her mind. She was obviously in a deep state of denial.

"Can I get you a cup of coffee?" Mrs. Montoya asked, getting up from her chair. It was obvious that she didn't want to continue this conversation anymore.

"No, thank you, Mrs. Montoya," I said, standing up. "I'm on my way home. I just wanted to stop by to let you know that I'm willing to help in any way I can." Then I reached inside my pocket for my business card. "I'll leave this with you," I said, placing it on the coffee table. "It has both of my telephone numbers. If you change your mind, please call me."

Mrs. Montoya thanked me politely and then walked me to the front door. As I pulled my car away from the curb, I noticed that María was watching me from an upstairs bedroom window. I waved goodbye to her, feeling very sorry for Mrs. Montoya and her entire family.

NINE
Tommy

The morning Mom comes to pick me up at the hospital, we both try to act as if everything is like it was before. Mom doesn't ask me any questions and I don't say much about anything except to reassure her that I'm feeling fine. Amanda is so excited to see me that she talks all the way home. For once I'm glad, because I don't have to say much of anything.

When we get home, I'm relieved that Dad is still asleep. Mom insists that I go straight to my room and lie down while she fixes me some *caldo de pollo,* chicken soup. Mom thinks that *caldo de pollo* is the cure for everything.

In my room, I lie back on my pillow and stare aimlessly at the ceiling. My mind keeps going back to the day I took the pills, but everything is blurry and confusing. I keep hearing Tyrone's question inside my head, "Are you a faggot or what?" By now, I'm sure rumors have spread all over the school. How will I ever be able to face anyone again? I don't know exactly what I'm going to do now. I close my eyes, hoping to find a magic solution in the darkness of my mind.

I'm half-asleep when María comes into the room. "Tommy, are you still sick?" she asks, sitting on the edge of the bed next to me.

I sit up. "No. I'm fine. What do you want?"

"I bought you a new Batman comic book while you were gone," María says, handing it to me.

"Thanks," I tell her, feeling surprised that she has bought me a comic book. I'm always yelling at her to stay away from my comic-book collection. I used to let her borrow my comic books, but I stopped because she left them all over the house and she never remembered to put them back in their plastic wrappers.

"I read it already," María says with a sneaky smile as I start to flip through the pages. "It's really good."

Amanda suddenly comes bouncing into the room, telling us that it's time to eat some *caldo.* As I force myself up from the bed to follow María downstairs, I glance at the clock on my nightstand, hoping that Dad is still sleeping. But since María's already home from school, he's probably awake.

When I walk into the kitchen, Dad is already sitting at the table eating. He's wearing his dull, gray janitor's uniform. As soon as I sit down next to María, he asks, "*¿Cómo estás, hijo?*" Before I can answer, he tells my mom, "Better give him a lot of *caldo, vieja.* He looks thin."

Mom quickly hands me a bowl of *caldo.*

"*Otra tortilla, vieja,*" Dad orders. Then he turns to look at me and asks, "When are you going back to school, Tomás?"

Mom immediately steps in and answers for me, "He has permission to stay home until Monday."

"Better make sure you get caught up with your schoolwork," Dad warns me.

"Yeah, I will," I answer in between mouthfuls, hoping he'll hurry and leave or that Amanda will spill her milk so that he will forget all about me.

"*Bueno*," Dad finally says, standing up, "gotta go." He grabs his lunch box from the counter, then goes over to the stove and gives Mom a kiss goodbye on the cheek. As he walks out of the kitchen, he calls back to María, "Don't eat so much, *gorda*." María wrinkles her nose at him while Amanda starts to tease her about being fat.

After Dad leaves, I can feel the tension in the room start to disappear. Mom serves herself some *caldo* and then she sits down in the chair across from me. "Are you feeling better, *hijo?*" she asks.

"I'm fine, Mom," I answer impatiently. "Would you please stop asking me every five minutes?"

A sad look appears on Mom's weary-looking face and I know that I've hurt her feelings. I suddenly feel guilty. Yet I want her to know that I don't want to be treated like a sick baby. "I guess I'm not that hungry," I say, pushing my plate away from me. Then I hurry back up to my room before Mom has time to say anything else to me.

✏ ✏ ✏

I spend most of the weekend in my room reading comic books or drawing. It's not easy, but I manage to avoid Dad entirely. He doesn't bother me, probably because he thinks I'm recuperating. Or maybe he thinks I'm doing the makeup work Mom brought me from school. Sometimes, Mom pokes her head in my room to ask me if I want to go somewhere with her and the girls, but I tell her that I have too much studying to do. By the worried look on her face, I can tell that she knows I'm lying, but still she doesn't try to pressure me.

On Monday morning, I know I have no other choice but to go back to school. As soon as I walk into my first-period class, I can hear students whispering around me. After Mr. Reiner signs my attendance slip, I hurry and take my seat in the back of the room, pretending I don't care that I'm the center of attention. While Mr. Reiner lectures on the Civil War, I doodle on my notebook paper. I imagine that I'm far away. I imagine that I'm someone else. Maybe this way I can make everything all right.

During second period, I almost jump out of my seat when they call my name over the intercom, asking me to report to the counseling office. As I get up to leave the room, I overhear Tim, one of Roosevelt's dumb football players, ask the girl sitting next to him, "Is it true he tried to do himself in?" My blood starts to boil and I want to turn around and smack him. But I don't. I hurry out of the classroom toward the main office, feeling angry and embarrassed.

When I walk into the counseling office, Mr. Belchor, the 11th grade counselor, comes over to greet me. He's a short, bald-headed man everyone makes fun of because of his last name.

"Hello, Tommy," he says. "Let's go in my office."

I follow Mr. Belchor inside his office and he closes the door behind us. I've only been inside Mr. Belchor's office once before. Most of the time the counselors at Roosevelt don't seem to care about talking with us Chicanos and Blacks.

"Tommy," Mr. Belchor begins, "is there anything you want to talk to me about?" I can tell that Mr. Belchor is nervous because he keeps fidgeting with the papers on his desk.

"Not really."

"I see," Mr. Belchor says, finally looking up at me. "Are you getting all your makeup work done in your classes?"

"Yes."

"Good," Mr. Belchor says. Then the room becomes silent while Mr. Belchor waits for me to say something else. When I don't, he asks me one more time, "Tommy, are you certain there isn't anything you want to talk about?"

I insist that everything is fine. But the concerned look on Mr. Belchor's face let's me know that I haven't convinced him. "Tommy," Mr. Belchor begins, "I want you to know that if you ever want to talk about what happened, I'm here to help."

For a brief moment, I want to tell him that I'm not okay, but instead I mumble thanks to him. Before I leave, Mr. Belchor hands me a small booklet, telling me to please read it. I thank him again. As I make a quick exit, the bell rings to change classes.

On the way over to my Algebra class, I glance at the booklet Mr. Belchor has given me. In bold letters, it reads: **Teen Suicide, Facts, Myths, and Prevention.** This isn't about me, I tell myself, flinging it into the nearest trash can before anyone can see me with it. Just as I am about to enter the Math building, David calls out my name, signaling me to wait for him. I flash him a dirty look and hurry through the door before he has time to catch up with me. At the end of the hallway I spot Rudy and Tyrone. They're standing against the lockers talking to a couple of girls I don't recognize. As I walk past them, Rudy whispers something to one of the girls and they all start to giggle.

When I walk inside my Algebra class, Ankiza right away says hello to me, and I mumble something back to her. During Mrs. Allen's lecture, I can feel Ankiza watching me. When Mrs. Allen asks me a question, I pretend I don't know so that I won't have to go to the blackboard.

By the time I get to Art, my head is bursting and I feel lonelier than I've ever felt in my life. I feel like people I don't even know are talking behind my back. Maya comes over to me and tries to cheer me up.

"Hi, Tommy," she says. "I've missed you."

"Oh, yeah?" I say, slowly taking my drawing out of my backpack.

"Are you okay?" Maya asks me gently.

All of a sudden, I reach down and crumple up my self-portrait. Then I grab my backpack and race out of the room before Maya has time to react.

TEN
Tommy

That Monday afternoon I cut all my classes.
And the next day, too. Every morning I get up like
always and pretend that I'm headed for school.
Mom never suspects anything and Dad is always
sleeping. I hang out at Snowball's, where I spend
most of the day drinking beer with him and his
buddies. I'm always careful to make sure that no
one sees me going in and out of his apartment.
Sometimes Snowball scolds me for not being in
school, but half the time he's so drunk that he
doesn't make sense. His friends don't seem to care
either, as long as I'm getting loaded with them.

I don't go back home until I'm sure that Dad
has left for work. Sometimes I catch Mom watching
me suspiciously out of the corner of her eye, but she
never asks me any questions. She leaves me alone
in my room where I pretend that I'm busy studying.

✎ ✐ ✐

By Friday, I'm feeling real panicky about cutting classes and lying to my parents. I start to
imagine all kinds of horrible things. What if the
school were to call my house and tell Mom that I've

been absent all week? What if I get so behind in my classes that I don't get to graduate next year? That same morning, I make up my mind that I'm not going to cut classes anymore. But before I head downstairs, I sneak a few drinks from the bottle of vodka that Snowball's friends gave me yesterday. Afterwards, I hide it underneath my books in my backpack. Then I hurry downstairs and run out the door before Mom even notices.

I take the long way around to Roosevelt so that I won't run into Rudy and Tyrone. When I get to the football field, I go over by the bleachers where no one can see me and pull the bottle of vodka out of my backpack. I sneak a few more drinks before I put it away. Then I write myself an excuse so I can be readmitted, forging my mom's signature.

In between my second- and third-period class-es, I go in the boy's bathroom and take a few more drinks. Then I pop a stick of gum in my mouth so that no one can smell the liquor on my breath. By the time fourth period rolls around, I'm feeling a lit-tle buzzed. Just as I am about to head down the hallway to Art, I meet up face-to-face with Maya.

"Tommy," she gasps. "Where've you been? I've been calling and calling you at home, but you won't take my calls."

Aware that my voice is slurred, I start to answer, but my backpack slips off my shoulder and falls to the floor. As I bend down to pick it up, I suddenly lose my balance, but Maya quickly reaches over and grabs me by the arm to steady me. There is a look of horror and shock on her face.

"Tommy, are you drunk?" she snaps at me.

I know I've been busted. I know that Maya can smell the liquor on me. "Yeah, so what?" I answer rudely, leaning against the wall.

"Tommy, don't be that way with me," Maya says with a hurt look in her eyes. "You know I'm your friend."

"Oh, yeah? You like queers or what?" I tell her sarcastically.

"Don't be stupid, Tommy. You know I'm not like Rudy and Tyrone or all those other jerks. I broke up with Tyrone 'cause of the way he treated you."

"Why'd you do that?" I ask sullenly.

"I think he's an ignorant pig, just like Rudy. I told Tyrone that I can't understand how he can be prejudiced himself when so many people are already prejudiced against us Chicanos and African Americans."

All of a sudden, the walls start spinning around me and my legs feel wobbly. "God, I feel so dizzy," I mumble as the tardy bell rings in the background.

Maya immediately hooks her arm through mine and says, "Come on, let's go. If a teacher catches you like this, you're in deep trouble."

I let Maya lead me out of the Liberal Arts building and through the inner quad. The fresh winter air feels good, and my head starts to clear a little.

"Where are we going?" I ask Maya as we walk past the gym toward the parking lot.

"We're going over to Foster Freeze. You can get some coffee there and sober up."

"I don't want you to get in trouble for cutting classes."

"Don't worry. I can take it," Maya says, smiling.

✎　🖎　✑

It only takes us about fifteen minutes to get to Foster Freeze. The snack bar is empty except for an elderly couple busy reading the newspaper. I keep my distance from the waitress so she won't smell the liquor on me while Maya orders a large coffee and a Coke.

When our order is ready, we sit at the booth farthest to the back, away from the elderly couple. Maya orders me to drink some coffee. I take a few sips. Then she asks me point-blank, "You've been cutting classes all week, haven't you, Tommy?"

I nod my head, wondering how the heck I'm supposed to drink this horrible tasting liquid when I can't even stand the smell of it. I think about my dad and how he has to drink tons of it so he can stay awake all night.

"You know you're going to get caught, Tommy. Sooner or later the school's gonna call your mom and dad."

"Yeah, I guess so," I answer Maya, staring straight ahead at the tired-looking woman with two small children who has just walked in. The room is suddenly filled with noise, and I think about my two little sisters and how I've been ignoring them lately, chasing them out of my room.

"Tommy, you know that I'll always be your friend, right?" Maya asks, leaning forward so I can't avoid looking directly at her.

"Yeah, I guess," I answer in a quivering voice. "But what about everybody else?"

"Who cares about everybody else, Tommy. They act like a bunch of jerks, anyway."

This time I manage to force a smile. Maya is always so dramatic.

"Tommy, will you do a big favor for me?" Maya reaches over and places her hand over mine. "Will you talk to Ms. Martínez?"

"What for?" I feel frightened again, of myself, of the truth.

"Remember last semester when my parents went through the divorce and I thought I wasn't going to make it? I felt just like you did. I hated everything. I wanted to run away from everything, but Ms. Martínez really helped me. She talked a lot to me and helped me."

I remain quiet, thinking back to the night Ms. Martínez came to see me at the hospital. I guess I was pretty cold to her.

"Come on, Tommy. I know she can help you."

I shrug my shoulders. I want to believe Maya. I want to believe that somebody can help me so that I won't feel so miserable. "Do you really think so?" Suddenly, I'm overcome by fear at the thought of telling a complete stranger how I feel. "I don't even know her."

"You'll like Ms. Martínez. She's cool, not like most adults. What if I go and call her right now from the phone booth? Maybe she can see you right now?"

Before I have time to protest, Maya is standing up. "I'll be right back," she tells me. I watch in disbelief as Maya disappears out the door and across the street to the phone booth.

My head starts to fill with scary thoughts as I wait for Maya to return. What if Ms. Martínez doesn't want to talk to me after the way I acted with her that day? Or what if she calls my mom and tells her stuff about me? Nervous and full of crazy thoughts, I lay my head down on the table and close my eyes, hoping to shut out the entire world.

A short while later, Maya comes back and triumphantly announces, "Tommy, guess what? I talked to Ms. Martínez and she can see you in a half-hour. Her office isn't far from here. Don't worry, we'll walk over there together."

I have no choice but to mumble, "Okay," hoping that Maya won't notice how terrified I'm feeling.

ELEVEN
Ms. Martínez

After I hung up the phone with Maya, I hurried out of my office to the kitchen in the back to hunt for some food. My office and that of two other therapists was housed in an old Victorian mansion, and we liked to keep snacks on hand for moments like this when an unexpected patient interrupted our lunch hour.

As I rummaged through the refrigerator, I thought about Maya's surprise phone call. Just last night I had found myself wondering how Tommy was getting along at school. From my conversation with Maya, he wasn't doing well at all, just as I'd expected.

After settling on some peach yogurt, I fixed myself a cup of herbal tea and headed back to my office where I curled up in an armchair to wait for Maya and Tommy. It had been a very hectic morning. I'd had to squeeze in several walk-ins I'd never seen before. New patients were particularly draining. It was always difficult trying to get them to talk. And just when I thought I'd finally get a break, Maya called. Oh, well, as Frank always reminded me, life in the fast lane wasn't easy.

I was just about to move over to my desk when I heard the buzzer ring at the front desk. Slipping my shoes back on, I hurried out to the reception area where I found Maya and Tommy waiting for me. While Maya appeared to be perfectly at ease, Tommy seemed very uncomfortable. He kept shifting his weight nervously from one foot to the other.

Maya's face broke into a big smile as soon as she spotted me. "Hi, Ms. Martínez," she said cheerfully.

"Hello, Maya," I said, coming up to her and giving her a hug. "How's that old professor-mom of yours?"

"Oh, she's fine," Maya answered.

I turned away from Maya to look directly at Tommy. "Hello, Tommy. I'm glad you came."

Tommy mumbled hello to me and, although his face wasn't as pale as when I had last seen him in the hospital, there was a glazed look in his eyes. It was probably from all the alcohol he had consumed this morning. My heart went out to him, and for an instant I wanted to reach over and embrace him, hold him tight, tell him everything would be all right. But I knew that I couldn't. I had to be careful, take it slowly, maintain my distance.

Maya's voice suddenly interrupted my thoughts. "Tommy, I'll wait right here for you, okay? I have tons of homework to do."

A look of panic crossed Tommy's face and for a moment I thought he was going to bolt right out of the door. But instead he nodded his head in agreement. Before he had time to change his mind, I instructed him to follow me down the hallway to my office. As soon as we walked inside, I showed Tommy to the blue armchair and the comfortable couch across from my desk. I told him to choose either one. After a few awkward seconds, Tommy took a few steps forward and let his slight body sink into the couch.

While I waited patiently in my chair for Tommy to begin speaking, I could feel the tension building inside him. I decided it was time to break the ice. "Maya has told me what great friends you both are."

"Yeah, I guess so," Tommy muttered, turning to gaze out the only window in my office.

Hoping to get Tommy's complete attention, I leaned forward in my chair and said, "Tommy, I want to reassure you that anything we discuss here is confidential. It's between you and me, and it won't leave this room."

Tommy continued to gaze sadly out the window. After a very long minute, I spoke again, "Tommy, I know that things have been pretty rough for you lately."

Tommy turned to look at me with those desolate green eyes that reminded me so much of my brother's. "Maya told me how you helped her and Juanita, but I don't think you can help me."

"And why do you think that?" I asked gently, feeling grateful that I finally had his attention.

"No one can help me. My problems are hopeless."

In the gentlest voice I cold find, I asked, "Won't you give me a chance, Tommy?"

Tommy suddenly lowered his head, not saying anything for a few moments. Just as I was about to speak, Tommy looked up at me and blurted out, "I'm so sick and tired of all the pretending. I'm sick of the way my mom acts. She acts as if nothing ever happened, as if I never tried to kill myself. She even lied to Dad about it."

"Why do you think she did that?" I asked, knowing all too well the answer to my question.

"'Cause she's stupid, that's why. She's afraid of my dad. She's always been afraid to stand up to him."

"Sometimes the truth can be just as frightening for adults," I said, remembering all those long and lonely years that my own family had tried to hide the truth about Andy's death.

"Well, I can't take it anymore," Tommy said, lowering his head again. "Sometimes I just want to end it all."

I reached over and placed my hand on Tommy's, telling him, "Tommy, I know that sometimes things can become so overwhelming that we feel we can't go on anymore. But I want you to know that you're not alone, that I'm here to help you in any way I can."

Tommy raised his head. "Have you ever felt like that, Ms. Martínez? Have you ever felt like life wasn't worth living?"

I gazed deeply into Tommy's grief-stricken eyes, remembering Andy's funeral. "Yes, Tommy, I have. But with the help of people who cared about me, I was able to get better."

"Yeah, but my problems are hopeless," Tommy said, blinking back the tears that were quickly clouding his green eyes.

"Nothing is ever hopeless, Tommy. Nothing."

There was a long silence as I watched Tommy fold and unfold his hands. Finally, he looked up at me and whispered, "I feel so ugly inside."

"Can you tell me why you feel that way?" I prodded gently.

Tommy inhaled deeply and in a voice barely audible, said, "I think I'm gay. That's why I feel so ugly."

It was finally out in the open. Tommy had revealed the terrible secret that had been eating him up inside. Maybe now we could get somewhere. Find some answers.

"I know Maya told you what happened at school," Tommy continued in a shaky voice. "...How everyone laughed at me, how Rudy called me a queer."

"Yes, Maya told me what happened."

"Now everyone at school is treating me like I have AIDS or something. And I feel so ashamed. I feel like running away, but I don't know where to go." Tommy leaned forward, burying his face in his hands in a futile attempt to hide the tears that were starting to slide down his face.

I reached over and handed Tommy a Kleenex and patted him lightly on the shoulder. It was good for him to cry. It cleansed the soul, the spirit.

I waited until Tommy's tears had subsided then told him, "Tommy, there's nothing wrong with being gay. This world is made up of all kinds of people. It's all right to be gay."

Tommy stared at me intensely, "Do you know anyone who's gay, Ms. Martínez?"

I wanted to smile at the absurdity of his question, but I knew that I shouldn't. "Of course I do. My brother-in-law, Bryan, is gay. He's a great human being. And I have many other friends who are gay and lesbian. They're all great people, too."

"My dad's always making jokes about gays. He says they're nothing but *jotos.*"

"A lot of people feel that way, Tommy. But they're wrong. They just haven't been educated properly."

I watched as Tommy fought to keep the tears from coming out. "I'm so tired of lying about who I am," he whispered. "The only thing I want is to be treated like everyone else."

"Is that why you tried to take your life, Tommy?" I asked gently.

"Yeah. I just couldn't take it anymore. And then when I went back to school, everyone was making fun of me so I started cutting classes and getting high."

"And has that made you feel better?"

"At first it did, but then things seemed to get worse. Now I'm so confused I don't know what to do. I really want to graduate, go to college. I don't want to end up like my dad, working as a custodian all my life."

"Don't worry, Tommy. We'll make sure you graduate. But the first thing you need to do is to stop drinking and get back in school. Do you think you could talk to your parents and tell them how you've been cutting classes?"

A frightened look appeared on Tommy's face. "No way. If I told my Dad, he'd kill me."

"How about your mom? Can you talk to her?"

Tommy hesitated for a moment before he answered my question. "Yeah, I guess I could tell Mom."

"It's important that you to talk to her right away so that she knows what's been going on. Do you think you can do that this week?"

Tommy quietly nodded his head.

"And, Tommy," I continued, "it's also very important that you talk about your feelings, about everything that's happened. How would you feel about getting together with me once a week just to talk, here in my office?"

"I don't know," Tommy answered reluctantly. "My parents don't have any money."

"Don't worry about that, Tommy. The money's not important. What's important is that we get together to talk about your feelings. Would you like me to call your mom and tell her about this?"

There was a moment of silence while Tommy sorted out a response to my question. "No, that's okay, Ms. Martínez. You don't need to call my mom. I'll tell her we're gonna start meeting."

"Good," I said, glancing at my watch. There were only five minutes left until my next appointment. "Now, how does next Tuesday at 3:30 sound?"

"Yeah, that's good."

"Will you be all right until then?" I asked, getting up from my chair.

"Yeah, Ms. Martínez. I'll be all right. I know it was a mistake to take all those pills." There seemed to be a glimmer of hope in Tommy's eyes.

This time I didn't resist the impulse. I reached over and gave Tommy a quick hug before I walked him back out to the reception area.

TWELVE
Ms. Martínez

When I arrived home that evening, I was surprised to find Frank's car already parked in the driveway. Before he had left for his office that morning, Frank had reminded me that he wouldn't be home until after dinner. January was always the beginning of the busiest time of year in the accounting firm where Frank worked. They were starting to get people's taxes filed before the deadline. It wasn't unusual for Frank to work until way past eight o'clock, which meant I often ate dinner alone. And if there was anything I disliked, it was eating alone.

As soon as I opened the front door, I called out Frank's name, but he didn't answer. Thinking he might be cooking dinner, I flung my briefcase on the floor next to the couch and went to look for him in the kitchen. Occasionally I would arrive from work to find Frank cooking one of three things: spaghetti, grilled cheese sandwiches or greasy potatoes with ground beef, a dish he had learned from my mother.

When I walked into the kitchen, I found Frank sitting on a chair with the telephone receiver in his hand. He glanced over at me, and the serious expression on his face warned me that something was wrong. Not wanting to interrupt his conversation, I kissed him lightly on the cheek then walked over to the refrigerator for my usual can of Pepsi. As I headed back into the living room, I heard Frank say, "Yes, Mom. Don't worry. I'll call him this evening."

A few minutes later, Frank came into the living room and sat next to me on the couch. It was unusual for Frank to be so quiet. He was usually full of silly jokes and remarks from the minute he walked in the door.

"Frank, what's wrong?" I asked. "Was that your mother on the phone?"

Without uttering a single word, Frank reached out for me and buried his head in my shoulder.

"Honey, what is it?" I insisted, running my fingers through his thick curly hair.

Frank finally raised his head to look at me, revealing a sad expression in his sea-blue eyes. "It's Bryan. He's in the hospital."

I felt a cold shiver race through my body. I knew how close Frank was to his older brother Bryan. It was Bryan whom Frank had always admired and sought out for advice.

"What happened?" I stammered. "Is Bryan all right?"

"He's in the hospital. He has a severe case of bronchitis," Frank explained. His voice faltered for a moment before he was able to continue. "Mom said he's going to be fine, but they found out he's HIV positive."

Now I understood Frank's pain. Tears filled my eyes and I reached out for Frank. We sat holding each other tightly for a few minutes. When we finally let go of each other, I felt safe and secure again.

"I told Mom I would call Bryan tonight. I guess he's known about it for a while, but he didn't want anyone in the family to know. He kept it a secret from us because he was afraid of how we'd all react."

My mind raced back to my conversation with Tommy and the secret he had been carrying around for so long. Secrets. First Tommy. Now Bryan. Another of life's endless ironies.

Frank's voice brought me back. "I can't believe Bryan didn't tell me about it. We've always been so close."

"I'm sure he didn't mean to hurt you, honey," I said, hoping to soothe him. The anguished look on Frank's face saddened me. "He was probably trying to spare you some pain."

"But I've always supported him, ever since he first came out and told us he was gay. I can't understand why he thought this would be any different."

There were tears in Frank's eyes. I put my arms around him again and said, "I know, honey, but maybe he had a lot of things to work out with himself first. Finding out you're HIV-infected can be very frightening. Many people keep it a secret for fear of losing their jobs, their families, and even their friends. Just be thankful that Bryan was able to tell the family now. Does your sister know?"

"Yes. Mom said she called Kim last night. I guess she took it pretty hard."

"That's understandable. How are your mom and dad taking it?"

"I guess they're fine, but Mom sounded pretty sad on the phone. Do you think he's going to die?" Frank suddenly blurted out.

"Oh, honey," I said, caressing his cheek. "That's the wrong way to think. Many people who are HIV positive live healthy, productive lives. And if I know Bryan, he's not going to let something like this stop him."

The tiny creases that had formed on Frank's forehead disappeared as he leaned back against the couch, letting his body relax. "You're right, Sandy. It's just that, well, it's all pretty scary."

"I know, honey. It'll take time for everyone to adjust to the news. Do you want to call Bryan right now?"

"No, that's all right. I'll call him after dinner."

"I know what will cheer both of us up," I said, standing up. "How about if we order Chinese take-out? Anyway, we're both too exhausted to cook. How about it, *guapo*?

"Okay, sexy," Frank answered, smiling. "Call the order in and I'll go pick it up."

✎   ✐   ✎

An hour later, after we had finished stuffing ourselves with Chinese food, Frank turned to me and said, "I guess I better call Bryan."

"I'll be here if you need me," I said.

"Don't worry," Frank said, heading for the kitchen. "Us macho guys are tough."

Sometimes Frank picked the weirdest times to make a joke. Oh, well, I thought to myself. At least, he was trying to be cheerful in the midst of such a difficult phone call. It was always painful bringing things out in the open for the first time. My thoughts drifted to Tommy and how brave he'd been today, openly discussing his feelings about being gay. Yet, it was scary knowing he'd attempted to take his own life. The suicide rate among teenagers

was so high, and I didn't want Tommy to be another
statistic like Andy.

I was staring blankly at the T.V. when Frank
came walking back into the living room. The peace-
ful look on his face told me that his phone call with
Bryan had calmed him.

"How did it go?" I asked as Frank sat down
next to me.

"We had a good talk. Bryan says he's feeling
great. That he's going home tomorrow. Diego was
there."

"I'm so glad Diego's there with him," I said,
remembering the first time I had met Diego. It was
Christmas Day and Bryan had shown up at his parent's house with Diego, casually introducing him as
his lover. It had taken awhile for Frank's parents to
get over the unexpected shock of meeting Diego, but
Frank and I had taken an instant liking to him,
especially me. Since Diego and I were both of Mexican ancestry, we ended up having a lot to talk
about. That had been five years ago, and now everyone in Frank's family treated Diego as part of the
family.

"Bryan says he doesn't want anyone to visit
just yet," Frank sighed. "But he'll let us know as
soon as he's ready. He said we can have a long talk
then, so I guess I'll have to wait."

"I think it's important to honor Bryan's wish-
es," I agreed.

"But he said he's worried about Mom. I guess
she took the news pretty hard."

I was suddenly filled with empathy for Frank's
mother. All her money and conservative ideas
wouldn't spare her the pain she was experiencing
right now. I promised myself I would try to be more

compassionate with her the next time we visited them.

"Bryan asked for you. He said to tell you it's nice to know there's a shrink in the family he can turn to if he ever needs one—free, of course."

"Didn't you tell him I'd have to charge him double since he's related to my mother-in-law?" I teased back.

Frank grinned. "Now, Sandy, you know how much you love my mom!" We both started to laugh, and I was pleased that Frank was feeling better.

✎   ✐   ✎

Later that night, I had the same dream I'd had many times before. We were living in the old farmhouse. I could see myself tiptoe quietly from one room to the next searching for Andy. When I finally came to his room, Andy was lying in bed with the covers pulled tightly over his face. Frightened, I approached the side of his bed and quickly yanked the covers back from his face. I heard myself scream. But this time it wasn't Andy lying there with his face all rotted. It was Bryan.

THIRTEEN
Tommy

I'm glad I took Ms. Martínez's advice and told my mom about the days I ditched. At first, Mom got real mad and yelled at me, but afterwards she said she was happy I told her the truth because she didn't want me to get kicked out of school. Then she lectured me about how I'll be the first one in the family to graduate from high school. When I mentioned to Mom that Ms. Martínez wanted me to meet with her once a week in her office, she nodded her head quietly and asked me how much it would cost. I told her that Ms. Martínez said not to worry about the money. Even though Mom didn't say anything, I knew she was glad I had agreed to meet with Ms. Martínez.

Walking over to my Algebra class, I come up to a group of students who are standing by the girls' bathroom talking. I recognize the tall blonde girl who is in my History class. They start talking in hushed voices when they see me coming. The only one who says hello to me is the blonde girl, whose name I don't even remember. I mumble hello and hurry past them, but not before I hear one of the guys tell her, "Watch out, Susan. Don't you know he's a faggot?" Embarrassed, I hurry away down the hallway and I don't slow down until I finally get to Algebra. During class, I'm glad that Mrs. Allen doesn't ask me to work a problem on the board, because I'm too upset to concentrate during the entire period.

By the time I get to Art class, I'm feeling pretty depressed and I look forward to losing myself in my artwork. Mrs. Grant is extra nice to me today. Before I even sit down, she calls me over and tells me I can start a new self-portrait.

As soon as I sit down, Maya points to her drawing of Frida Kahlo and asks, "How do you like the monkey?"

I stare at Maya's drawing for a few seconds and then tell her, "The monkey's almost as hairy as Frida!"

Maya punches me in the arm and we both start to laugh.

The rest of the period goes by quickly as I busy myself with my new self-portrait. I draw different parts of my face as if they were fragments of a mirror, all broken up into small pieces. When Mrs. Grant walks by, she pauses to compliment my work, which makes me feel pretty good inside.

When the bell rings, I gather up my supplies and head out the door and down the crowded hallway. Maya is right behind me.

"Tommy, let's have lunch together," she says, coming up next to me. I'm about to tell her okay, when we run right smack into Tyrone, Rudy and Juanita, who are standing next to the water fountain.

Maya slows down to talk to them, and I can feel Rudy staring at me. As I walk past them, I hear Rudy tell Maya, "What are you doing with the *joto*?" I want to turn around and slug Rudy, but instead I

hurry away as fast as I can in the direction of the
library. When I get there, I find a table way in the
back where I can be alone. Then I lay my head
down and close my eyes, wishing I could disappear
off the face of the earth. All of a sudden, I feel someone tap me on the shoulder. I raise my head to find
Maya standing next to me.

"Come on, Tommy. Let's go eat," she says.

"Why don't you eat with your friends?" I answer
in an angry voice.

"With those jerks? Don't let them get to you,
Tommy. They're just a bunch of idiots."

"That's easy for you to say, Maya. They all like
you."

"That's what you think! Anyway, I don't care
what other people say. Come on, Tommy, let's go eat.
I'm starved," Maya insists, pulling at my sleeve
until I finally get up and follow her out of the
library.

After we stop at our lockers, we find a quiet
spot behind the main quad where there aren't too
many students hanging around.

"Here, I saved this for you," Maya says, handing me her Ding-Dong.

"No thanks, " I answer, feeling dark and dreary
like the gray clouds hanging over us.

"I'm sorry Rudy's such a creep," Maya says.
"But Juanita's not that way. It's just that she's all
hung up on Rudy, or else she'd be here eating with
us. And Tyrone's acting like a jerk, too."

"It's not just them, Maya," I blurt out. "It's the
whole damned school. They call me names behind
my back. They act as if I've got AIDS."

"Don't listen to them, Tommy. They're all ignorant and they're not worth it."

"I don't know if I can take it, Maya," I say, lowering my head.

Maya reaches over and squeezes my hand. "Sure you can, Tommy. I'll be right here with you. Don't ever forget that, okay? I'm your friend, and so is Kizer."

I stare into Maya's chocolate-colored eyes and I remember what Ms. Martínez said about Maya being one of my best friends. "Thanks, Maya," I whisper.

"Now, quit feeling sorry for yourself and eat," Maya orders. Somehow she manages to make me smile.

✎ ✐ ✏

After school, I can't resist going by Snowball's apartment, even though I told Ms. Martínez I'd try to stop drinking. But when I get there, the drapes are drawn and no one answers the door. I have no choice but to go home.

As soon as I step inside the living room, Amanda comes running up to me. "Look at the bird I made," she says, proudly handing me a sheet of paper that has something on it that looks like a huge blob of red paint.

"What kind of a bird is it?" I ask.

"A red bird," she answers. Then she grabs it out of my hand and disappears into the kitchen.

I glance over at Dad, who is sitting in the armchair watching television. He's wearing one of his plaid flannel shirts instead of his gray janitor's shirt, which means it must be his day off.

"How was school today?" he asks me. But before I can even answer, he hollers out to my mom in the kitchen, "*Vieja*, bring me a cup of coffee."

Then he turns back to look at me, wanting an answer to his question.

"It's fine," I lie, noticing that his face is more haggard and the bags under his eyes have gotten bigger. For a fleeting moment, I almost feel sorry for him.

A Bud Light commercial comes on and they show a sexy brunette waiting on two cowboys in a bar. Dad lets out a whistle, telling me to check her out. I pretend to stare at the T.V., but as soon as Mom comes walking in the room with his cup of coffee, I escape upstairs.

I stay in my room listening to the radio and thinking back to my day at school. I know that if it weren't for Maya, I don't know how I would make it at school. She's the only real friend I've got. Awhile later, I'm half-asleep when María comes into my room and announces that dinner is ready. I hurry downstairs, knowing that Dad doesn't like us to be late for dinner.

When I walk into the kitchen, everyone is already sitting at the table. As soon as I sit down next to Amanda, Mom starts to serve me some chicken. I grab the platter out of her hand, saying, "I can serve myself."

But Dad immediately steps in and says, "*Déjala*, Tomás. That's woman's work."

I ignore him, but he keeps right on talking to me. "*Hijo*, I think it's time you and I had a talk about girls."

I can feel my face turning red. María looks at me and says, "Do you have a girlfriend, Tommy?"

"Shut up," I tell her.

"Of course he does. Not one, but two. Right, *hijo?*" Dad says, winking at me.

It takes all of my will power to keep from throwing my plate at him. Sensing how embarrassed I've become, Mom comes to my rescue. "*Viejo*, my *comadre* Marcela called last night. She's having problems with her clutch and she was wondering if you could take a look at her car this weekend?

"Tell her I'll look at it on Saturday," Dad answers, shifting his attention to cars. Then he starts telling Mom in detail about the time he single-handedly replaced my *tío* Pedro's clutch.

When Amanda and María start arguing about who gets to watch what program on T.V., I quickly excuse myself from the table.

"Is that all you're going to eat, *hijo*?" Mom asks with a worried look. Dad tells her to leave me alone, that I'm not a baby anymore.

Back in my room, I stare at the comic books on my bookcase, wishing that I were strong and invincible like Batman. Maybe then I could stand up to my Dad, to everybody.

FOURTEEN
Tommy

After school the next day, I don't feel like facing my dad, so I decide to go hang out at Snowball's apartment until I'm sure Dad has left for the hospital. This time the curtains are wide open, and as soon as I knock, Snowball opens the door. His eyes are bloodshot and his hair is all messed up, but the only thing I can think of is whether Snowball has any booze. The funny thing is that I don't even like the taste of alcohol. When I ask Snowball for a drink, he points to the bottle on the floor next to the couch.

During the next few hours, I have several shots of vodka while I listen to Snowball talk about his life back in Colorado, where he was born and raised. When I ask Snowball where he got his nickname, he explains that when he was little, he liked to play in the snow. One day one of his uncles started to call him "Snowball," and the name kind of stuck to him. Snowball's eyes fill with tears as he mentions his family. I feel sorry for him. I'm sorry that he's all alone in this crummy apartment.

By the time I finally get up to leave, I know that I've had too much to drink because I'm light-headed and the room is spinning around me. Before

I leave, I hand Snowball a five-dollar bill, telling him to lie down for a while because he's pretty plastered by now. Snowball just nods his head sadly and takes another drink.

As soon as I get home, I carefully make my way over to the stairway, hoping to escape upstairs before anyone notices me. But before I even climb the first step, Mom comes out of the kitchen and walks right up to me. "Tomás, where have you been?" she asks angrily.

Steadying myself on the railing, I hear myself tell her in a slurred voice, "I had to stay after school."

"*¡Mentiroso!* You stink like alcohol," Mom says, grabbing me by the arm.

María and Amanda hurry over from the kitchen to see what's happening, but Mom orders them to go upstairs to their room. Then she pulls me into the living room, insisting that I sit down on the couch next to her. "Who gave you the alcohol?" she asks angrily.

"What do you care, anyway?" I lash out.

"*Hijo*, what do you mean by that? Don't you know how worried I've been about you ever since that day?"

I feel a volcano erupting inside of me. I'm so tired of hiding the truth, of lying. My eyes start to get watery as I explode, "Don't you want to know why I did it, Mom? Why I tried to kill myself?"

A look of terror appears on Mom's face, but I know that I can't stop, that I have to go on. "I did it because I'm tired, Mom. I'm tired of hiding the truth from you, from everyone."

"What truth, Tommy?"

I stare deeply into Mom's eyes and I hear myself whisper, "That I'm gay, Mom. That's what it's all about. I'm gay."

Mom's face turns deathly pale. After about a minute, she finally manages to speak. "You don't know what you're saying, Tomás."

"Yes, I do, Mom. I've known it for a very long time."

The next thing I know, Mom gets up from the couch and takes off to her bedroom. I hear her slam the door behind her. As I slowly climb the stairs to my room, María appears at the top. With an angry look on her face, she asks me, "Why'd you make Mom cry? Were you being mean to her?"

"None of your business," I yell at her as I go into my room.

✎   ✐   ✎

That night, I feel as if a terrible burden has been lifted off my shoulders. But the next day, I start to feel guilty for telling Mom the truth. Although she doesn't mention it again, I can tell that she's feeling miserable. Her eyes are red and swollen and she's quieter than usual. And when Dad finally notices and asks her what's wrong, I overhear her tell him that she's coming down with the flu or something. But the following evening, Mom sends the girls to bed early and calls me into the living room to talk.

"*Hijo*," she beings nervously, "I talked to Father Steve and he wants to talk with you about your problem. He says that with the Lord's help you can be cured."

I can feel the anger slowly mounting up inside me. I can't believe my mom is saying this. I thought if anyone would understand, it would be her. But I guess I was wrong. I want to swear at my mom, hurt her just like she's hurting me right now. But I don't. Instead, I get up and leave, slamming the door behind me.

I go straight to Snowball's, where I sit and drink until I'm so loaded that I pass out. By the time I wake up, it's past midnight, and I know that I have to get home before Dad finds out I've been out all this time.

As soon as I walk through the front door, Dad comes up to me and starts yelling at me. Then he slaps me hard on the face. *"Desgraciado joto,"* he hollers at me. Get the hell out of my house." Mom is standing behind him, crying. "Get your things and leave. I won't have a *joto* in my house."

In shock, I slowly step around him. "No, Tomás, *por el amor de Dios,"* I hear my mother cry out as I climb the stairs. In my bedroom, I hurry and throw some clothes into my backpack, wondering what I'm going to do now. Then I hurry back downstairs. Dad is sitting on the couch, his body slumped down. He looks up at me as I head for the door. For a moment, I feel as if he wants to stop me from leaving. But I don't give him a chance.

"Don't worry, I'm out of here," I yell at him. The last thing I hear as I shut the door behind me is a loud moan coming from my mom.

FIFTEEN
Ms. Martínez

As soon as Tommy stepped inside my office, I knew that things hadn't been going very well for him. There were dark circles under his eyes and when he sat down, his body seemed to pull him down like a dead weight. Once again, I resisted the urge to reach over and cradle him in my arms like I used to do with Andy.

"Well, Tommy, how have you been since we last talked?" I began.

Tommy hesitated for a moment as if he weren't quite sure how to respond. Then he let out a deep sigh as he said, "Not so good."

I waited patiently for Tommy to continue while I watched him nervously fidget with the zipper on his backpack. As the silence in the room mounted, I finally spoke up.

"Are things worse at school?"

Tommy raised his head to look at me. "Not so much at school." There was a short pause and then he continued, "My dad kicked me out of the house last night."

Now I understood why Tommy was looking so depressed. I'd been afraid that things might blow up in his face. "Can you tell me what happened?" I pried gently.

Tommy breathed deeply then explained in detail the events of the night when he arrived home drunk to find his dad waiting for him.

"He said he didn't want a *joto* in his house," Tommy concluded, tears filling his green-speckled eyes. "I've been staying at Maya's house since then."

"I'm so sorry, Tommy. I know how this must hurt," I said, feeling the anger mount inside me. It wasn't fair that Tommy had to go through this, but I also knew that he wasn't the only one. I remembered what Frank had told me about how it had taken his dad almost fifteen years to come to terms with the idea that his oldest son was gay.

"To tell you the truth, Ms. Martínez, I'm glad it's out in the open. I'm sick of all the lies. And I don't care if Dad hates me. He makes me sick anyway."

"Your dad doesn't hate you, Tommy," I tried to explain, leaning forward in my chair. "Deep down inside he loves you, but he's feeling confused. He's probably in shock. When parents suddenly find out that their children are gay, it takes them time to adjust to the idea that their children aren't what they expected."

"I don't care what he thinks," Tommy answered belligerently. "I'm never going home again as long as he's there. Maya's mom said I could stay with them as long as I need to. She's been real nice."

"I'm glad you feel comfortable at Maya's," I said, thinking to myself that if anyone knew the agony of what parents went through with their kids, it was Sonia. After all, it wasn't too long ago that Maya had tried to run away because of Sonia's divorce.

"But it's kind of hard not being home," Tommy said, looking away toward the window. "I miss my little sisters a lot."

"Tommy, is there any possibility you might be able to sit down and talk with your parents about what all of you are going through?"

Tommy gave me a long hard stare. "Not with my dad. No way. The only person he listens to is himself. Mom says he was raised like that, but she likes to make excuses for him."

"I don't think it's an excuse, Tommy. In traditional Mexican culture, men are raised to be real machos. And many times the mothers are conditioned into accepting that behavior. Many of them even raise their sons like that."

"Yeah, I guess so, but that doesn't make it right."

"No, it doesn't. But at least it helps to understand where this attitude comes from."

I waited for a few minutes while Tommy thought about what I had just said. Finally, I decided it was time to discuss his drinking problem. "Tommy, you said you were loaded the night you had the fight with your dad and that you've kept going over to Snowball's after school. I think this is something serious we need to talk about. Drinking doesn't solve anything."

Feeling uncomfortable with my reference to his drinking problem, Tommy started to fidget with his backpack again. "I don't know why I drink. I don't even like the way alcohol tastes. I guess it helps me escape."

"Escape what, Tommy? Being gay?" I asked. It was important that Tommy talk openly about being gay. He needed to stop avoiding the real issue and get his feelings out in the open before he destroyed himself.

"Yeah, I guess so. Everyone at school hates me. They call me queer or faggot behind my back. It makes me so angry. Maya's the only one who's nice to me. But she's not around all the time. Then my mom. She thinks it's the devil's curse or something. She was trying to get me to go see a priest to see if he could cure me."

Tommy was crying softly now. I handed him a Kleenex and waited for him to get a little control before I continued.

"I'm sorry, Tommy. People can be very cruel. And I know it's hard to believe this, but the way your mom reacted is very typical. Just as you have to go through your own coming-out process, so do parents. It takes time for parents to understand that being gay is not a choice, that being gay is who you are and that there's no shame in being who you are."

"And then I always thought that if any of my friends stood by me, it would be Rudy and Tyrone 'cause of all the prejudice we've been through at Roosevelt. But I was dead wrong." Tommy let himself slouch down on the couch, blinking back the tears that kept forming in his eyes.

I reached over and patted him on the hand and said, "Tommy, one of the things that you need to remember is that people can be very ignorant. It takes time, education and awareness for them to change their beliefs. But those friends who really do care for you will come around in time, and those who don't, well, they aren't worth your friendship, anyway, because they don't love you for who you really are."

I remembered how Frank had told me that some of his aunts and uncles still refused to mention Bryan's name, let alone be in the same room with him.

"Do you think it's wrong to be gay, Ms. Martínez?" Tommy asked, interrupting my thoughts.

"No, Tommy. It's not wrong to be gay. How can it be wrong to be yourself? There's no shame in being who you are."

Tommy breathed deeply, releasing some of the tension from his body. I leaned back in my chair and reached over to the far right-hand side of my desk. "Tommy, I want you to read this," I said, handing a book to Tommy. "It's called *Straight Talk for Gay Teenagers*. I hope it will help answer many of your questions. It's a good book and it's helped a lot of teenagers like you." While Tommy quietly leafed through the book, I retrieved another book from my desk. "And there's one more thing I'd like for you to do," I said, handing it to him. "I know this might sound silly to you, but I'd like you to try writing down your feelings for me in this journal. It might seem like a strange request, but, believe me, it'll help."

"I don't know, Ms. Martínez," Tommy said. "I'm not much for writing."

"Why don't you think about it, okay? I know you like to draw, so you can even sketch as you go along. But the important thing is that you keep track of your feelings. Will you try just for me?"

"Okay," Tommy finally agreed. "I'll try it."

"Great," I said as the buzzer rang, letting me know that it was time for my next client.

As Tommy got up to leave, I noticed that his face looked brighter and more hopeful. Before he

left, I gave him a small hug and remind him to call
me at home at any time if he needed to talk.

SIXTEEN
Ms. Martínez

That evening, Frank and I were halfway through our dinner when the doorbell suddenly rang. "Are you expecting someone?" Frank asked in an irritated tone.

"No," I answered wearily as Frank got up from the table. "I sure hope it's not some obnoxious salesman."

A few moments later, I heard an unfamiliar voice speak to Frank. I hurried out to the living room only to be completely taken by surprise at the sight of Tommy's mother standing in the entryway.

"Hello," I greeted Mrs. Montoya, trying not to sound too surprised.

"Hello, *Doctora* Martínez," she said, clutching her purse tightly against the bulky red coat she was wearing that made her smaller and heavier. "I hope you don't mind, but Maya's mother gave me your address."

"Of course not. Please come in. You already met my husband?" I said, glancing at Frank.

A faint smile appeared on Mrs. Montoya's dark brown face, but the anguished look in her eyes told me that she was feeling very nervous and uncomfortable. Sensing that we needed to be alone, Frank politely excused himself and went back to the kitchen.

"Please sit down, Mrs. Montoya," I said warmly, pointing to the couch.

Mrs. Montoya sat down and immediately began to speak. "I'm so sorry to show up like this at your home, *Doctora* Martínez, but I didn't know what else to do, and you said if I ever needed anything to call you, so I decided to come over."

"It's no problem at all, and I'm very glad that you came."

"It's about Tomás," Mrs. Montoya said, her voice cracking. Then all of a sudden, she was crying, and tears were streaming down her face. I quickly moved to her side and put my arm around her. When Mrs. Montoya's tears had subsided, I handed her a Kleenex.

"I always suspected, ever since he was little. He was never interested in what boys like, but I never wanted to believe it. I guess I thought he'd grow out of it. And now, I don't know what to do."

"Don't worry, Mrs. Montoya," I calmly reassured her. "Everything will be fine."

"I always hoped Tomás would get married, have children. I don't understand what we did wrong. Maybe it's his dad's fault. He never spent a lot of time with him. I don't know. Maybe it's God's fault." Mrs. Montoya's voice faltered and she was crying softly again.

"Mrs. Montoya, it's not your fault nor your husband's," I said firmly. "It isn't anyone's fault."

Wiping the tears from her swollen eyes, Mrs. Montoya looked up at me and said, "The only thing I know for sure is that I want my son back. I don't care if my husband kicked him out. I want Tomás to come back home."

"I know you do, Mrs. Montoya. And I know how difficult this is for the whole family. Finding out that your son is gay can be quite a shock. Most parents have certain expectations of their children, and when things don't go as planned, they react with anger and confusion."

"I feel so ashamed. And I'm so afraid of what everyone in the family will say when they find out. I can't seem to think straight anymore," Mrs. Montoya whispered.

"I'm so glad you came to talk to me, Mrs. Montoya," I said. "The way you're feeling is quite normal. Some parents in your situation completely reject their children; others ignore the truth and simply tolerate their kids. But many parents do learn to love and accept their children for who they really are inside."

Mrs. Montoya stared helplessly at me and said, "I love my son. I will never reject him. But I don't know anything about gays or whatever he says he is."

I patted her hand lightly. "That's an important first step, Mrs. Montoya, admitting that you don't know anything about your son's homosexuality. Tommy is feeling confused, too, and he's going to need all your love and support to come to terms with being gay."

"My husband will never accept this," Mrs. Montoya warned. "For him, it's the worst thing possible, like a disease or something."

"You have to give your husband some time, Mrs. Montoya. Sometimes it takes fathers a longer time to come around. But for now, let's deal with your own feelings."

"I sure hope you're right, *Doctora* Martínez."

"The first thing I want to suggest is that you sit down and talk to Tommy straight from the heart. Tell him exactly what you told me. He needs to know that you still love him for who he is inside. Talk about your feelings. Let him know that you're just as afraid as he is because you don't know anything about homosexuality."

"What if he won't listen to me? His dad and I already hurt him so badly. He refuses to come home."

"Then you keep trying until he does listen to you. Tommy is hurting inside, and he needs to hear you say that you love him despite anything that's already happened. For all he knows, you feel the same way his dad does."

Mrs. Montoya sighed deeply. "Yes, *Doctora* Martínez. I'll go over to Maya's house as soon as I can and talk to him."

"And I want you to do something else for me, Mrs. Montoya. I want you to read a book that will help you understand what being gay is all about. I also have some pamphlets from an organization called PFLAG, Parents and Friends of Lesbians and Gays, that provides support for parents like yourself. Let me get these for you."

"*Gracias*," Mrs. Montoya said as I headed for the bedroom in the back that served as an office for Frank and me.

When I returned with the book and pamphlets, Mrs. Montoya's face seemed more relaxed. The tightness around her mouth had disappeared and her forehead seemed more relaxed. "Keep these as long as you need them, and if you have any questions, please let me know," I said, handing her the books.

Mrs. Montoya thanked me again. Then she stood up to leave, explaining that she needed to hurry back to pick up the girls who were with a neighbor. I gave her a warm hug and reminded her to come over anytime she needed to talk.

As I closed the door behind her, I felt a dull pain somewhere deep inside as I thought of my own mother. If only she had been able to talk about our family problems, like Mrs. Montoya was attempting to do, instead of keeping them hidden away in some dark corner. Maybe then Andy would still be alive.

SEVENTEEN
Tommy

Driving home Sunday night with Mom, we don't say much to each other. We're both silent, afraid that if we say anything else, things might change, that I might decide it's a mistake to go home. I didn't think I'd ever be going home again. I mean, I swore to myself that I wouldn't, but then, I never thought my mom would talk to me the way she did tonight. It had surprised the heck out of me when Maya's mom told me that Mom was waiting to talk to me in the living room.

When I walked into the room and saw her sitting on the couch, I wanted to turn around and go back to the bedroom. But Mom's face looked so sad that I knew I couldn't hurt her like that. Mom immediately pleaded with me to sit down next to her, that she had something important to tell me.

"Tomás, *hijo*," she began, "I went to see *Doctora* Martínez the other night, and we talked a lot. She was real nice; she gave me some books to read."

My first reaction was to get even for all the pain she and Dad had already caused me. When I accused her of coming to see me only because Ms. Martínez had told her to, Mom quickly defended herself. "*Hijo*, please give me a chance to explain.

I'm not here 'cause anybody told me to come. I'm here because I love you and I want you to know that I'll always love you, no matter what."

Startled by her sincerity, I had responded sarcastically, "Do you really mean that or are you just saying it? You don't think I need to see a priest anymore, so he can cure me?"

Mom's eyes filled with tears. "No, *hijo*, you don't need to see a priest. I'm sorry if I hurt you when I said that. It was dumb of me to think that. I know that God made everybody different. I want you to know that I love you for who you are, Tomás. The only thing I want is for us to be a family again. I want you to come back home. We all need you—I need you, your sisters need you."

I thought about what Mom had just finished saying. Then I remembered Dad and how angry he had been the night he kicked me out of the house. "What about Dad?" I asked her.

"Me and your father already talked. I told him that if you couldn't come home, that I was going to leave him."

I couldn't believe what I was hearing. Mom had never stood up to Dad before.

"The girls and I really want you to come home. Anyway, your dad knows how I feel."

"I don't know if I can take being around him," I responded, my voice trembling.

There was a brief silence while Mom wiped away the tears that were falling down her cheeks. Then she exhaled slowly, saying, "*Doctora* Martínez says she thinks your dad will change with time. She says it's always harder for dads to accept this."

The next thing I knew, Mom reached over and held me tightly in her arms. A short while later, I gathered up my things, thanked Maya and her mother for letting me stay with them, and went out to the car with Mom, relieved that I was finally going home.

✎ ⬚ ✐

When Mom and I get home, Dad is sitting in the living room watching television with a can of beer in his hand. He doesn't say a single word. He doesn't even turn to look at us, but I don't let it get to me. After all, I'm glad to be home again. As I walk into the dining room, Amanda comes running up to me. I bend down to hug her and she tells me, "Tomás, you want to see the picture I drew you?" But before I can answer her, María, who is right behind her, quickly interrupts, "Tommy, I'm glad you're home." Then María hands me a new X-Men comic book, saying, "I got this one for you."

"Thanks, *gorda,*" I tell her, blinking back the tears.

When I take off upstairs to my room, María and Amanda are right behind me. This time I don't chase them away. I let them follow me inside.

"How come you left us?" Amanda asks, sitting next to me on my bed. "It was lonely without you."

I reach over and ruffle her hair.

"Why? Is María still picking on you?"

María, who is busy looking at the comic books on my book shelf, glances over at me and says, "She's nothing but a crybaby."

"No, you're the crybaby," Amanda defends herself, but María tells her to shut up.

I smile to myself. It's so good to be back home. Hoping to get my sisters to stop fighting, I ask if they want to play *lotería.* This is the one game that the three of us like to play together when I'm in a good mood. María nods her head yes and Amanda right away jumps off the bed and goes to her room for the game. I can tell by their reaction that they've both missed having me around. It was kind of fun being at Maya's house, it's so big and modern, but there's nothing like being home with my own family.

We play *lotería* until Mom calls us for dinner. María and Amanda hurry downstairs, but I take my time, hoping that Dad will finish eating before I get there. No such luck. When I walk into the kitchen, he's seated at the head of the table with María on one side of him and Amanda on the other. "Tomás, *siéntate acá,*" Mom says, pointing to the chair next to her plate. As I sit down, Dad glances at me, but he doesn't say a word. There is a strained look on his face, and I know he's feeling as uncomfortable as I am. Even Mom is nervous. She keeps going back and forth from the table to the stove, asking Dad if he needs another *tortilla.*

I pick at my food, trying hard not to look across the table at Dad. He hasn't said a word since I sat down. When María starts to tell me about this mean boy in her class who pulled her hair today, Dad tells her to be quiet and eat. María stops talking right away. By the time Mom sits down at the table, Dad has finished eating. He pushes back his chair and gets up, asking Mom to get him another beer, even though he's only a few feet away from the refrigerator. I can feel my blood start to boil.

As soon as Dad has left the kitchen, the tension in the air starts to disappear. Mom seems more relaxed as she tells us about what's happening in her new *novela* on T.V. When María accidentally eats some *chile jalapeno*, we all laugh. She jumps up from the table, gasping for air, and rushes to the sink for some water. I tease her that maybe now she won't talk as much as she does. "*¡Olvídalo!*" Mom says, and we all laugh again.

Back in my room that evening, I take out the journal that Ms. Martínez gave me. I stare at a blank page for the longest time until I finally decide to write something down:

Dear Me,

It's not easy being me. Sometimes I really hate myself. And sometimes I wonder who I really am inside. I don't know why God made me this way. It hurts so much being who I am. I don't even know if it's right or wrong. Sometimes I wish so badly that I could change myself, but I know that I can't. I can only be me—Tommy. I can't be anyone else. Why can't my friends understand this? Why can't people love me for who I am. Why can't Dad try to understand me? I wish I could be like everyone else. It hurts so much being who I am. I don't mean to hurt my friends or my family. I just want to be loved for who I am.

Tommy

EIGHTEEN
Tommy

The minute I walk into Art, Maya signals for me to hurry to where she's sitting. As I come up to her, she holds up her finished portrait of Frida Kahlo.

"Well, what do you think?" she proudly asks.

Placing my backpack on the desk next to her, I answer, "Don't you think her eyebrows could to be a little bushier?"

Maya's face breaks into a big smile. She punches me playfully in the arm.

Then Mrs. Grant announces that everyone should get busy, so I sit down, carefully taking my self-portrait out of my backpack. I'm busy shading in the final pieces when Maya leans over to look at it.

"That's really coming out good, Tommy."

"Thanks," I answer, hoping Maya will leave me alone so I can finish it.

"How were things at home yesterday?" Maya asks.

I'm not sure how to answer her because I'm still not convinced that I did the right thing by going home. "It was okay," I finally say, unwilling to take my eyes off my drawing. "Mom was pretty cool and my little sisters were happy to have me back."

"How about your dad?"

"No change." I try to sound as if I don't really care.

"Don't worry, Tommy, he'll come around. When Mom and Dad got a divorce, Dad acted like a real jerk with me, but now he's pretty cool."

I'm just about to tell Maya that my problem with my dad is much more serious than hers when Mrs. Grant comes walking up behind us.

"Maya, are you bothering Tommy again? Don't you need to start matting your portrait?"

Maya shrugs her shoulders and quickly takes off to the back of the room to look for matting materials. Mrs. Grant moves up closer to examine my work. After a few seconds, she says, "I like it very much, Tommy. It's very original. You might think about entering it in the Spring Art Contest."

I want to tell Mrs. Grant that the last thing I want to do is share my feelings with the entire school, let alone the whole town, but instead I mumble, "Thanks, Mrs. Grant. I'll think about it."

As soon as Mrs. Grant leaves, Maya reappears with two different colored mattings, insisting that I help her pick between the gray and the black. I answer, "The black one is better 'cause it'll match her bushy black eyebrows!"

Maya sticks her tongue out at me as she turns and goes back to the matting area.

When the lunch bell rings, Maya tells me that she's eating lunch with me today. When I ask her if she isn't eating with Juanita and the rest of the group, she says, "Nope. I'm eating with you. Let's go over by the library where we ate the other day."

We're heading out of the Art building when Ankiza comes running after us. "Wait for me!" she hollers, out of breath.

Maya slows down so that Ankiza can catch up with us, but I don't. Embarrassed, I keep on walking, hoping they'll change their minds. But no such luck. It only takes a few seconds before they catch up to me.

"Hi, Tommy," Ankiza says. "Mind if I eat with you guys?"

I hesitate. I would like to tell her yes, I do mind. But when I look up at Ankiza, I feel an instant warmth. Her dark eyes are filled with kindness and I know that I don't want to hurt her feelings. After all, maybe she's like Maya. Maybe she's still my friend.

"Sure, it's okay," I answer, hoping I won't regret it.

Having lunch with Ankiza and Maya turns out to be the best part of my day. Even though it's cool outside, we sit on the grass next to the library. The first few minutes I'm a nervous wreck and I don't say much, but after a while I join in the conversation. We talk about movies and rap music, and by the time lunch period is over, I realize that Ankiza still thinks of me as one of her friends.

✎   ✐   ✐

After school, I'm feeling so good that I decide to walk home the old way instead of taking the long way around. As I turn the corner and head down Palm Street, I notice that Rudy and Tyrone are walking a few feet ahead of me. My heart starts to pound rapidly and I'm not sure what I should do. If I cross to the other side of the street, they'll spot me immediately, and if I don't, I'll catch up with them in a matter of seconds since they're walking very slowly. Determined not to let them ruin my good day, I decide to quicken my pace and pass them quickly. As I hurry past them, not daring to look their way, Tyrone calls out to me, "Hey, Tommy." Then I hear Rudy say, "There goes the faggot." I'm about to turn around and tell Rudy exactly what I think of him when I hear Tyrone tell him, "Leave him alone, you dumb *cholo.*"

The rest of the way home, I'm upset with myself again. If only people would leave me alone, let me be who I am. All of a sudden, I find myself heading toward Snowball's apartment. When I get there, I stare at his front door for a few minutes, unsure of what I should do. I feel compelled to go to his door and knock to find some relief for the pain I'm feeling inside. But then I remember what happened the last time I got drunk. I think about what Ms. Martínez said, that getting drunk doesn't solve anything. I quickly turn around and head back to my apartment.

When I walk into the living room, María and Amanda don't pay much attention to me because they're busy watching cartoons. I'm glad that Dad's already left for work. As I start to climb the stairs, Mom pokes her head out of the kitchen to greet me, and I mumble hello to her. Then I head straight for my room.

A few minutes later, I'm lying face down on my bed, feeling miserable and alone, when I hear a light knock on the door. "Who is it?" I snap, turning over on my side.

"*Hijo*, it's only me," Mom answers softly. "Can I come in?"

"Yeah, sure," I answer, sitting up against my pillows.

When Mom comes into my room, I notice she's still wearing her stupid red apron. Just once I wish I could come home and find her wearing something nice. But that would be a miracle because she's always busy cooking or cleaning up after somebody.

"Tomás, is something wrong?" she asks, sitting down on the edge of the bed. Her face is tired-looking and there are worry lines all across her forehead.

Suddenly, I realize what she might have imagined when I rushed up to my room. Horrified, I tell her, "Mom, you don't need to worry. I won't ever try anything stupid like before with pills or anything."

An instant look of relief appears on her small round face. "Good, *hijo*," she says, breathing deeply. "But I can tell that something's bothering you."

I look away from her, staring blankly at the posters on my wall.

"Tomás," she says, reaching over and patting my hand. "I want you to know that I'll always love you no matter what. And if there's ever anything you want to talk about, I'm right here for you."

My eyes fill with tears as I turn to look into Mom's eyes. "Sometimes I just can't take it," I tell her, my voice trembling slightly.

"What's wrong, *hijo*?"

"It's my friends. They hate me. They call me awful names."

"I'm sorry, *hijo*."

"I wish they'd just leave me alone," I say, lowering my head.

"I know it's hard, Tomás. But there's good and bad people everywhere. You have to learn to ignore people like that. When I was in school, a lot of kids used to call us all kinds of names to our face—spics, dirty Mexicans, greasers. Some of my friends used to get so mad that they'd start fights over it, but it just made things worse. I learned to ignore all the dirty words they called me even though it hurt badly, and it did. But I stayed close to the friends I knew really liked me. The rest, I didn't bother worrying about."

I stare at Mom for the longest time without saying anything. This is the first time she's ever told me something so personal about her life. I never realized how much harder it must have been back then growing up Mexican and poor.

"I know that Maya really likes you, Tomás, and I'm sure there's other kids who feel like her."

"Yeah, I guess so," I say, remembering Ankiza and how nice she was to me today.

"Then don't worry about what the others say, *hijo*. Ignore them. Sooner or later, they'll leave you alone. And maybe someday they'll understand. Your dad too. He's a stubborn old man, but one of these days he'll come around."

"Thanks, Mom," I whisper, reaching over impulsively and hugging her. Just then, Amanda comes racing into the room crying, "Mom, María pinched me!"

María, who is right behind her, snaps back, "She pinched me first!"

Mom and I look at each other and start laughing.

NINETEEN
Tommy

The next day, I'm standing at my locker when Tyrone comes walking up to me. I feel myself break into a sweat as I think about whether I should turn and walk away from him. But before I can make my move, he says, "Hey, Tommy. Can we talk for a minute?"

"Sorry, I can't," I answer coolly, walking away from him down the packed hallway.

But Tyrone doesn't take no for an answer. He hurries after me, grabbing me by the arm. "Look, Tommy, I just wanted to tell you that I'm sorry. I know I acted like a real creep and I'm really sorry."

Dumbfounded, I stare into Tyrone's eyes, not believing what I've just heard.

"Can we still be friends?" Tyrone asks.

I'm not sure whether I should believe him, but the look on his face tells me that he means what he's saying. "What about Rudy?" I ask, knowing that he and Rudy have been best friends for a long time.

"I told Rudy that he can go to hell if he doesn't like it," Tyrone answers in the self-assured tone I've always admired about him.

Just then the tardy bell rings and I'm glad for
an excuse to take off to class. "Sorry, I have to go or
I'll be late for Art."

Tyrone is persistent. "Me, Maya and Ankiza are
all going over to Foster Freeze at noon. Will you
come with us?"

Anxious to get away, I shrug my shoulders and
tell him yes.

Tyrone's face breaks into a big smile and as I
hurry away, he calls after me, "See you at noon at
the gym."

During Art class, I tell Maya about my conversation with Tyrone. She gets so excited that she
screams, "¡Orale!" out loud, and Mrs. Grant glares
at her. Then Maya tells me how happy she is that
Tyrone and I are talking again. I think about my
conversation with Mom the other night and how
she said real friends will stick by you no matter
what.

When the bell rings, I walk out of class with
Maya, promising her I'll meet her and the others at
the gym after I stop by my locker. A few minutes
later, I go to the gym where Maya, Tyrone and
Ankiza are waiting for me by the front entrance.
Feeling nervous, I mumble hello to Ankiza as we
begin walking across campus to Foster Freeze. On
the way, Maya and Tyrone do most of the talking.
Maya tells us that Rina has been missing a lot of
school lately and that she's wondering if something
is going on at her house. Then Tyrone changes the
subject and starts talking about last night's Laker
game.

It only takes us about ten minutes to get to
Foster Freeze. As soon as our order is ready, we sit
down to eat, since we only have about fifteen minutes left before lunch period is over. When Tyrone

asks Maya if she can help him with his Algebra homework, Maya looks at me and says, "Tommy's the Math brain. Why don't you ask him?"

Tyrone hesitates for a moment and then says, "What do you say, Tommy?"

A worried look appears on Ankiza's face as she waits to see how I'm going to respond to Tyrone's request for help. "Sure, come over tonight if you want," I answer. "Anyway, like Maya said, I'm the Math nerd!"

Tryone's face breaks out into a big smile, and we all laugh. Suddenly, it feels like old times. It feels like I have friends again.

After lunch, I'm walking across the inner quad to my fifth-period class when I see David walking in my direction. As he approaches me, David pretends to look past me, as if he hasn't seen me. But this time, I don't avoid him. I stop right in front of him and say hello. A puzzled look appears on David's face as he politely greets me back. Then I further surprise him by saying, "David, I have something I need to say to you."

"Yeah, sure," he stammers.

This time I don't care if anyone is staring at me while I talk to David. "I just wanted to say I'm sorry. I know I haven't been a decent friend lately. It's just that I've had a lot of things going on."

"Yeah, sure, that's cool," David says with a pleased look on his face.

"I just wanted you to know that."

"Thanks, Tommy," David says, smiling.

"No problem," I say, hurrying away toward the Science building.

✐   ▭   ✐

Later that night, lying in bed with my journal, I'm eager to write my thoughts.

Dear Me,

I guess it's not so bad being me. I guess I'm not such an awful person after all. Mom was right. My real friends will like me for who I am inside and that's all that really counts. Maybe Rudy and I will never be friends again. But that's all right. At least I still have some good friends left. I'm glad David understands what I've been through and I hope we can be friends like before. Sometimes it feels good to be me. It feels good to be alive. Okay, gotta go. Tyrone is coming over so I can help him with his Math.

Tommy

TWENTY
Ms. Martínez

By the bright look on Tommy's face, I knew he was in a better mood than the last time we had talked. Earlier in the day, I had spoken with Sonia and she had indicated that Tommy was back home with his mother. Eager to let him reveal his good news, I began, "Well, Tommy, how have things been since we last talked?"

"Pretty good," Tommy immediately replied. "I'm back home again. My mom showed up at Maya's house the other night and we talked a lot. She convinced me to go back home."

"That's very good news, Tommy. It seems like your mom is trying to be understanding, isn't she?"

"Yeah, I guess so. She told me she'll always love me no matter what. She even told me she's reading these books you gave her. Thanks, Ms. Martínez."

"You're very welcome."

A veil of sadness suddenly appeared in Tommy's eyes. "But Dad hasn't changed. I think he hates me. He never talks to me, not even when we're in the same room."

"Be patient, Tommy. Give your dad time to adjust. He's been through quite a shock, like your mom. Parents of gay and lesbian teens need time to go through their own coming-out process, just like their siblings. And it takes time. It doesn't happen overnight."

"Yeah, but it's hard being around him. I never know what he's thinking."

"I know it's difficult, Tommy, but try to be patient. I'm sure your mom will do everything she can to help smooth things out between the two of you. Now, how are things going at school?"

Tommy stared intensely at me and, after a few moments, he bowed his head and said, "It's still rough. It really hurts when people call me names. Sometimes I hate myself so much for being who I am."

I leaned forward in my chair and patted him gently on the hand. "Tommy, it takes each person a different amount of time before they finally come to terms with being gay. For some people, it takes years before they even think of coming out of the closet."

"It's really hard, Ms. Martínez," Tommy whispered, looking up at me. "I don't know if I'll ever accept the fact that I'm gay."

My heart went out to Tommy. I knew that he was in for some difficult years, especially since he came from such a traditional Mexican family. Yet, I had a feeling that with the right support systems, everything would work out for him. I would make sure he got the help he needed.

"But some of my friends are starting to act a lot nicer," Tommy said, interrupting my thoughts. "Tyrone apologized to me and asked if we could be friends again."

"And how do you feel about that?"

"It makes me feel really good. Tyrone's always been a good friend. But some of my other friends still won't have anything to do with me."

"I see."

"But I guess I have to learn to live with people like that. Mom said there were a lot of people who hated her when she was in school just 'cause she was Mexican, but she learned to ignore them."

"Your mom's absolutely right, Tommy. There will always be people who won't like you. But what really matters is that you accept yourself for who you are and that your friends do, too."

"Yeah, you're right, Ms. Martínez."

"Now, how about your other problem, the drinking?"

"I haven't had anything to drink in over a week," Tommy answered proudly. "One time, I almost went to Snowball's, but I decided it wasn't worth it."

"I'm so glad, Tommy."

"Yeah, me too. And I've been writing in the journal you gave me, Ms. Martínez. It really helps."

"Good. It always helps to write out your feelings."

"And the books you gave me to read helped a lot, too," Tommy added. He seemed slightly embarrassed.

"That's wonderful, Tommy. I also wanted to give you the number of a gay-support group at the university. You might think about attending sometime. It would be very helpful. They meet once a month."

"Thanks, Ms. Martínez. My friend David said they're talking about starting a gay-support group at Roosevelt High."

"That would be ideal. I'm sure glad someone raised the issue. If students can get together and show there's a need for such a group, the school administration will have to listen."

"I don't know what I would have done without Maya's help," Tommy suddenly blurted out.

"She's a very special person, isn't she?"

"Yeah, she's really stuck by me."

"I'm glad to hear that, because I think both you and Maya are very special people."

Tommy's face broke into a big smile that filled my heart with happiness. I knew right then and there that he was going to make it. There was no doubt in my mind whatsoever.

✐ ✐ ✐

By the time I arrived home that evening, it was already dark outside. I couldn't help but feel lonely knowing that Frank wouldn't be coming home that night. He had left early in the morning to spend the weekend in San Francisco with Bryan, and he wasn't driving back until Sunday. Diego was off somewhere on a business trip. I always hated it when Frank left me behind, but I knew how important it was for him to talk with Bryan alone. Ever since he had found out Bryan was HIV-positive, Frank had been on edge. He couldn't understand why Bryan had kept this a secret from him. Try as I might, I couldn't get Frank to understand that Bryan had his reasons for not talking about. Hopefully, this weekend Frank would be able to discuss his feelings with Bryan.

After I changed into my raggedy jeans and T-shirt, I went into the kitchen to make myself a ham sandwich. Then I grabbed my can of Pepsi and went to the living room to watch the evening news. As I watched one murder scene after another, I thought about Frank and how much he disliked the violence on T.V. I guess he was right. It was all too depressing.

I was busy clicking from one channel to another when the telephone rang. Hoping it might be Frank, I hurried back into the kitchen.

"Hello," I answered.

"Sandy, Hi, it's Sonia."

"Oh, hello. How are you?"

"Great. How about you?"

"Oh, miserable. Frank's visiting Bryan in San Francisco and I'm here all alone."

"*¡Ay, pobrecita!*" Sonia said. "Would you like to borrow Maya for a while? There's never a dull moment when she's around!"

"Sure, bring her right over," I teased back.

"You'll regret it!" Sonia said, laughing. It was nice to hear Sonia tease about Maya. For a while there, it had been touch and go after her divorce from Armando.

"Anyway, I was calling to ask if you'd like to go with me tomorrow to visit the AIDS Memorial Quilt. It's on display at the new gym on campus."

"Sure, I'd love to. I've been wanting to see it for quite some time now."

"So have I, and it's only here for this weekend. Why don't I swing by for you around nine-ish."

"That sounds good. We can have a cup of coffee together."

"Okay, I'll see you tomorrow," Sonia said.

I hung up the receiver, feeling pleased that I had something special to do this weekend instead of being miserable without Frank.

TWENTY-ONE
Ms. Martínez

On Saturday morning, by the time I crawled out of bed, showered and made coffee, it was almost nine o'clock. It was a good thing Sonia was running late because I hated to see anyone until I'd had my first cup of coffee. Unlike Frank who was always cheerful and making jokes in the morning, I was a real grouch until I had pumped some caffeine into my body.

As I drank my first cup, I wondered how Frank's visit with Bryan was coming along. I thought of calling him, but decided I should wait until he called me tonight. Knowing that Bryan was HIV-positive, was going to be rough on the whole family. I thought about how the AIDS epidemic was affecting everyone—women, children— and how teenagers were so much at risk. It was going to take a massive effort to educate our youth about safe sex and AIDS.

The sound of the front doorbell interrupted my thoughts. When I opened the door, I found Sonia looking very relaxed in a pair of blue jeans and a brightly colored blouse. Her long dark hair, which was pulled back in a ponytail, made her look more like a student than a college professor.

"Running on Chicano time?" I teased her.

"Of course, what did you expect?" Sonia said, stepping inside.

"I'm ready to go. Just let me grab my jacket," I said, opening the hall closet. "Where's Maya this morning?"

"She slept over at Ankiza's last night and won't be home until later."

"Sounds like fun to me," I said, putting on my jacket. " Okay, let's go. I'm anxious to see the Quilt even though I know it'll be depressing."

"I know exactly what you mean," Sonia replied as we walked out the door.

✎ ✐ ✐

Ten minutes later, we were on the university campus, which was located on the north side of Laguna. The parking areas adjacent to the Recreation Center where the AIDS Quilt was on display were all full, so we ended up parking several blocks away. On the way over to the Recreation Center, Sonia talked about one of her favorite Chicano professors from Stanford who had died of AIDS several years ago.

"He was my mentor and a great human being. We all loved him dearly," she said, teary-eyed. "He's on the Quilt and that's why I really wanted to come see it."

All of a sudden, I found myself telling Sonia about Bryan and how worried Frank had been lately. Sonia slowed down and gave me a quick hug, reminding me to call her if she could be of any help. It felt good knowing that I had a friend like Sonia, although we hadn't socialized much since her divorce from Armando, we still remained good friends.

When we came to the entrance of the Rec Center, there were several booths with volunteers who were handing out pamphlets on the AIDS Memorial Quilt and other information related to HIV and AIDS. I made it a point to pick up as many brochures as I could on teenagers and safe sex.

As soon as we walked inside the main floor of the gym, Sonia and I were overwhelmed by the beauty of the multi-colored panels that covered almost every inch of the floor as well as the walls. Sonia and I walked around speechless amidst the throngs of people who had come from all over the central coast of California to pay tribute to the people whose faces and names were on the panels of the quilt. It was heart-wrenching watching people cry for their sons, daughters, lovers, friends. There were several women on their knees writing special messages on the panels of loved ones. We were particularly moved when we came to Ryan White's panel, the young boy who had received national attention when he was denied schooling because he was HIV-positive.

After about an hour, we went upstairs to the second level to view the rest of the panels. When we arrived at the panel of Sonia's friend, she bent down and fondly caressed his picture. While Sonia cried softly, I examined the personal items that were sewn on his panel—an old high school ring, a picture of a young boy riding a blue tricycle, letters from brothers and sisters, and an old photo of a handsome teenager wearing a colorful Mexican sarape. My heart ached for Sonia and for our Latino community which was rapidly becoming one of the largest ethnic groups affected by HIV.

When Sonia and I finally left the Recreation Center, it took us awhile to regain control of our emotions. As soon as she was able to speak, Sonia asked if I would like to have lunch with her at the Faculty Club, and I immediately agreed.

By the time we had walked uphill to the Faculty Club, our somber mood had disappeared. We found a table near a window and I was instantly filled with a sense of calm by the breathtaking view of Ortega Peak.

"Isn't the view spectacular?" I asked Sonia.

"Yes, it's beautiful," Sonia answered. "Only I hardly ever get to enjoy it. Most of the time I eat in my office while I grade papers."

A tall, blond waiter appeared to take our orders. After he was gone, I turned to Sonia and asked, "How are things at home now?"

"Not bad," Sonia answered, revealing a faint smile. "Maya and I still have some things to work out. She still resents me for the divorce, but we're both trying to work at it. I remember when you told me that the first year's the roughest."

"That's absolutely true."

"But things are definitely improving for the both of us. Maya was ecstatic that Tommy agreed to go to the mall with her and some friends today. By the way, Sandy, is Tommy going to be all right?"

I hesitated. As a general rule of confidentiality, I never discussed my patients with other people. Yet, it was only natural for Sonia to ask about Tommy's welfare. After all, Sonia had taken Tommy in when his dad had kicked him out of the apartment. Like it or not, Sonia was indirectly involved and merited some kind of response.

"Yes, I think he's going to be fine. It won't be easy, but at least now he has some people to lean on."

"I'm so glad. I know how hard it is being gay in our macho culture. If there's anything I can do to help, please let me know."

"Thanks, Sonia, but I think Maya's friendship is the best help for Tommy. He really relies on her, you know that?"

"Yes, I know exactly what you mean. Maya's a great kid. Takes after her mom, right?" Sonia said with a mischievous twinkle in her eyes.

I couldn't help but smile back at her.

✎ ✏ ✐

After Sonia dropped me off at the house, I sat around and watched T.V. for a while. Then, feeling restless and bored, I decided it was time to do some housecleaning. When I finally finished vacuuming and dusting the entire house, I laid down on the couch with the new Danielle Steele novel Frank had bought me last week. Although Sonia liked to tease me about the junk fiction I read, it was very relaxing and made me forget about my patients and their problems. The only bad thing was that once I started reading a new book, I was hooked and had the hardest time putting it down. But today I welcomed the distraction, since I missed Frank terribly.

A short while later, I was just about to head over to the kitchen for my afternoon Pepsi when Frank came bursting through the front door.

"I'm back, gorgeous! Did you miss me?" he said, setting his overnight bag on the floor.

"Frank, you're home!" I sighed as he came over and pulled me into his arms.

We hugged and kissed as if we hadn't seen each other in months.

When Frank finally let go of me, I asked in a concerned voice, "What happened? Why are you home a day early?"

"Well, some of Bryan's friends invited him to Napa Valley for the day, and I told him to go ahead, that I was anxious to come home and be with you."

"That's so sweet of you," I said, giving Frank another long kiss on the lips.

"Gee, maybe I should leave more often," Frank teased.

"Don't you dare," I warned him. "How's Bryan? Did you two have enough time to talk?"

Frank's voice became very serious. "Yeah, we did. We talked for hours last night. We talked about HIV. I guess he's had it for several years, but he chose to keep it to himself. He said it took some time before he himself was able to come to terms with being HIV-positive."

"I can understand why."

"He said there were a lot of times when he wanted to call and tell me, but he was afraid. But now he's glad we all know. And he said he doesn't want anyone to treat him differently, that he's still the same Bryan. But I made him promise that if he ever needs anything, he'll call me."

"What about Diego? Has he been tested?"

"Diego's fine. He doesn't have the virus, which makes Bryan feel a lot better."

"Thank God."

"Bryan said to tell you hello and that when he's ready for more company, he'll let us know."

"Good. I'd love to see him and Diego."

"Now, tell me about your day," Frank said, gently running his fingers through my short black hair.

But before I had time to answer, he asked, "Are you hungry? There's a new pasta take-out over on Sierra Drive. How about it, sexy? *¿Vámonos?*" Frank asked.

"*Vámonos*, partner," I answered, mimicking Frank's accent and we both started laughing.

TWENTY-TWO
Ms. Martínez

I was just about to go to the little hamburger place a few blocks from my office when Tommy came walking through the front door.

"Hi, Ms. Martínez," he greeted me.

"Well, hello," I said, wondering what Tommy could possibly be doing here in the middle of the day. Our next appointment wasn't scheduled until the following week.

"Aren't you supposed to be in school?" I asked with a puzzled look on my face.

A smile quickly spread across Tommy's young face. "Yeah, I am, but I got permission to go off campus for lunch with my mom. She's in the car waiting for me."

I couldn't help but let out a sigh of relief.

"Mom and I wanted to surprise you. We'd like to invite you out for lunch today."

"What a nice idea," I said, smiling. Tommy's invitation to lunch was a perfect example of the generosity that existed in the *barrio* from families who had so little and yet gave so much. It was this warm-hearted generosity that made all my endless hours of giving to the Chicano community seem worthwhile.

"There's this new *taquería* on Mill Street and Mom thought you'd like it 'cause it's real authentic."

"Sounds good to me. Why don't I follow you there, that way I can run some errands on the way back, okay?"

Tommy nodded in agreement and we walked outside together. Before I climbed into my car, I casually waved to Mrs. Montoya, who was parked alongside the street. Then I carefully backed out of the driveway, pulling up behind Mrs. Montoya's blue Nissan.

As I followed Mrs. Montoya through Laguna's busy downtown streets, I was filled with a deep satisfaction thinking about how much better Tommy and his mother were getting along. It was obvious that Mrs. Montoya would do anything in her power to keep from losing her son.

When we turned onto Mill Street, I smiled as I spotted the new *taquería* Tommy had mentioned. It was a little hole in the wall, Frank's favorite kind of place. As soon as we parked, I got out of the car and went over to greet Tommy and his mother. Instead of politely shaking my hand, Mrs. Montoya surprised me by giving me a brief hug. As we walked inside the small *taquería*, I thanked Mrs. Montoya for inviting me out for lunch. She smiled at me and said, "Tomás and I wanted to thank you for everything you've done for us."

"You don't need to thank me for anything," I replied, glancing at Tommy who was looking embarrassed by our conversation. "I think you have a terrific son."

"*Buenas tardes*," the cashier greeted us as we approached the small counter. "May I take your order?"

"What do you want to eat, Ms. Martínez?" Tommy said teasingly. "They have *tacos de sesos, de lengua, de cabeza*. Take your pick!"

I let out a small laugh. "This is definitely where I need to bring Frank. He's a gringo who loves to taste all kinds of Mexican food. But I won't tell him what he's eating until he's finished."

Mrs. Montoya smiled, and Tommy started to laugh.

As soon as we finished ordering, Mrs. Montoya took out her wallet to pay. When I tried to intervene, she said, "No, *Doctora* Martínez, please let me pay. It's our way of showing how special you are."

I happily thanked Mrs. Montoya for her generosity. Then we walked to the back of the room and sat down in a booth next to the jukebox, which was playing loud *banda* music, the hottest type of Mexican music on the radio today.

While we waited for our tacos, Mrs. Montoya talked about Tommy's little sisters and how much they liked school. Then Tommy complained about how it drove him crazy that they liked to follow him wherever he went. When I finally asked Mrs. Montoya if her husband had changed his attitude toward Tommy, she looked at me sadly and said, "A little bit. The other night he actually said something to Tomás."

"That's good," I said.

"Yeah, he ordered me to get something for him, that's about it," Tommy explained.

Mrs. Montoya was quick to come to her husband's defense. "Before, he wouldn't even look at Tomás, but now I think he's trying."

"That's the right attitude to have. It's important to stay positive and give Mr. Montoya time to work things out for himself," I said, patting Mrs. Montoya on the hand.

"I'll never know how to repay you for helping my son," Mrs. Montoya said, her soft eyes filling with tears.

"Remember what I said, Mrs. Montoya, you don't need to pay me back for anything."

"*Gracias por todo*," Mrs. Montoya said, wiping away the tears.

The waiter suddenly appeared with a tray of tacos. Tommy immediately grabbed one and said, "Okay, who ordered the brain tacos?" And before I knew it, we were all laughing at Tommy's impromptu joke. I knew then, deep down in my heart, that Tommy was going to make it, just like Bryan, just like me and all those others who had overcome great obstacles.

TWENTY-THREE
Tommy

Dear Me,

Today was a good day. I had fun with my mom and Ms. Martínez. I don't know how tomorrow is going to be. Maybe I'll feel angry. Maybe I'll feel sad. But at least now I know that I won't have to stand alone anymore.

Tommy

Glossary

Ándale, hijo.—Go ahead, son.
arroz—rice
¡Ay, pobrecita!—Oh, you poor thing!

banda—band
Buenas tardes—Good afternoon
Bueno, vieja.—Okay, old lady (endearing).

caldo—soup
caldo de pollo—chicken soup
¡Cállate!—Shut up!
cerveza—beer
Chicano (a)—a person of Mexican descent living in the U.S. who has a political consciousness related to Chicano issues and those of other ethnic groups.
Chicanos—plural form of Chicano/a
chile jalapeño—jalapeño peppers
chismosa—a gossip
cholo (a)—modern-day Mexican/Chicano youth who dresses distinctively and rebels against mainstream culture.
cochino—pig
comadre—godmother, protector, friend, comrade
¿Cómo estás, hijo?—How are you, son?

Déjala, Tomás.—Let her do it, Tomás.
desgraciado joto—damned queer

¿Estás seguro?—Are you sure?
Estás bien loco.—You're really crazy.

flaco—skinny
Frida Kahlo—Mexico's most famous female painter (1907–1954).

gordo(a)—fatso
gordita—a chubby female
gracias—thank you
Gracias por todo.—Thanks for everything.
guapo—handsome
güero—a light-skinned or fair-haired person

hijo—son
¡Híjole!—Wow! My goodness! Oh my gosh!

joto (s)—queer

lotería—Mexican bingo

mentiroso—liar
m'ijo—the contraction of "my son"

narizón—big nosed
novela—short for "telenovela" or soap opera

¡Olvídalo!—Forget it!
¡Orale!—Hey!; Okay!; Right on!; All right!
otra tortilla—another tortilla

panzón—big bellied or fatso
pipí—pee pee
por el amor de Dios—for the love of God

¿Quieres algo, viejo?—Can I get you anything, old man?
¿Quihúbole?—What's up? What's happening?

ruca—chick, babe, homegirl

Sábado Gigante—a popular Saturday night variety show on Spanish television hosted by Don Francisco

siéntate acá—sit down here

taquería—taco stand

tacos de cabeza—tacos from the cow's head

tacos de lengua—tacos from the cow's tongue

tacos de sesos—Tacos from the cow's brain

tía—aunt

tío—uncle

tonto(a)—dummy

¡Tráeme una cerveza!—Bring me a beer!

¡Vámonos!—Let's go!

4⁰⁰   Gen 9/16 TP